THE HAUNTING OF BEACH HOUSE

MT EDEN WITCHES BOOK FOUR

JAMIE SANDS

GREY KELPIE STUDIO

978-1-0670421-7-2Haunting of Beach House (epub)

978-1-0670421-8-9Haunting of Beach House (paperback)

Cover design by Jacqueline Sweet

CONTENTS

1. Chapter One   1

2. Chapter Two   5

3. Chapter Three   10

4. Chapter Four   15

5. Chapter Five   19

6. Chapter Six   29

7. Chapter Seven   35

8. Chapter Eight   52

9. Chapter Nine   64

10. Chapter ten   78

11. Chapter Eleven   85

12. Chapter Twelve   96

13. Chapter Thirteen   114

14. Epilogue   121

Also by   128

CHAPTER ONE

BASIL

B asil opened the mailbox outside his front gate as a matter of habit, not really expecting to find anything. The envelope was a surprise. So much of a surprise that it almost fell out, but on instinct Basil's hand shot out to catch it. He lifted it to examine it closer.

It was a beautiful envelope, not too heavy with a linen feel to it. There was a handwritten address in deep magenta ink. It was addressed to Sebastian Black.

No stamp or return address when Basil checked, so it must have been hand-delivered.

Feeling watched, Basil glanced over his shoulder, but there was no one on the street in the late summer sun. His neighbour's familiar cars were parked where they always were, and over the road someone was weeding their garden and listening to headphones.

He made his way up the cobblestone path to the front door and let himself in.

Sebastian wasn't due back for a few more hours. He'd texted earlier to say he'd seen all he thought he would at the latest ghost hunt — one he'd been away for over night. He'd driven to the Waikato the day before to investigate and film at a possibly haunted Bed and Breakfast.

Basil had missed him, and hoped he wasn't taking too meandering a route home. The Bed and Breakfast had been pretty rural, and far from the Waikato Expressway that would have him home quicker. He always missed him, but now he was impatient for Sebastian's return so he could find out what was in the envelope.

He placed it in the middle of the dining table, sat down and gazed at it. With no return address, he couldn't even speculate at what it could be. It was sealed with wax which ruled out sneakily opening it to have a peek.

Not that he would open it. It was Sebastian's mail and Basil believed firmly in boundaries, but the temptation was there all the same.

Maybe he could speculate.

Perhaps it was something from Sebastian's rich and absent parents — a family wedding invitation?

It looked like a prop from some Gothic play. Maybe it was an invitation to one of those murder mystery dinner parties. Sebastian must know a hundred people who'd be into those although how many would know his home address?

Sebastian often got fan mail for his show — he was handsome and charming, he got a lot of fan mail. But it was always sent to his post office box and he only checked that every few weeks.

Whoever delivered this had known for certain he lived at this address, and Sebastian never shared that online.

Someone local maybe? Judith from up the road with her monster?

But anyone local would have addressed it to Basil as well, those were shared friends. Well, of course, everyone liked Sebastian better so perhaps it was something that Basil wasn't supposed to know about.

He picked it up again. He knew for certain it was an invitation of some sort. Some magic knowledge or intuition assured him of it. This wasn't a stalker letter or something threatening, he knew it in his gut.

So perhaps someone Sebastian knew, who didn't know Basil. This was the most simple explanation. It could be an invitation with a plus one. Sebastian made friends everywhere he went. It was one of the things Basil loved about him.

A creak in the ceiling shook Basil out of his reverie. He blinked, as if waking up. He'd come in and done none of his usual routines and rituals. In fact the front door was still standing open.

Basil went to close it, cleared his throat and called out.

"Hello, Eek! I'm home. Had a good day?"

The wall creaked, closer to Basil.

"Hungry are you?"

He went to the pantry, located a packet of chocolate digestives and arranged them on a plate on the sideboard. "Dinner's up, Eek."

Then he turned away, to give their house monster the privacy it preferred. He sensed the large shape moving closer, making the floorboards creak. How such a sizeable form fit into the walls, he'd never quite understand. Just one of those things you had to write off to magic, he supposed.

"Hello Basil, thank you." The whisper was part autumn leaves and part the rustle of raincoats hanging in a closet. Basil looked in the reflection of the kettle to get a glimpse of Eek. Eek ate delicately, distorted in the curved surface. Basil smiled, a wave of affection warming his chest.

"I thought this might be a good variation to your diet," he said softly. "More fibre."

"Mmm. Thanks."

The whoosh of movement told Basil that Eek had retreated, leaving only crumbs on the plate.

In a concerted effort to not sit back down and stare at Sebastian's envelope, Basil started making dinner.

He baked some potatoes, put together a large green salad with boiled eggs and cheese cubes, and marinated a slab of tofu.

Since Sebastian's cat curse, they'd been experimenting with a lot more meatless meals. Basil has questioned this, surely being a cat would make him want *more* meat but Sebastian had explained some of the urges that came with being a cat had lingered. He hadn't had the chance to eat a mouse when he'd been transformed, but apparently as a cat he had very much wanted to. Human Sebastian was repulsed by the idea of eating mice, so had been trying more tofu and vegan dishes to try and quash the instincts.

It had been months since then, and for the most part Sebastian was back to his old self. However, there was no denying his attitude to magic had changed. It was as if he'd never realised fire could burn, and then he'd scorched himself. To Basil's mind, a bit of caution was good, healthy. But Basil had felt himself walking on eggshells somewhat since their return.

Sebastian had left the room when Basil had refreshed the protective charms on the windows, and although he was still friendly with Eek, sometimes the noises the monster made startled him.

The summer hadn't been too hot, so Basil had spent a lot of time in the garden, leaving Sebastian to do his own thing.

But now, this envelope, addressed to Sebastian... Basil had a sense that things were about to become a lot more interesting, maybe even challenging. How would they cope?

CHAPTER TWO

SEBASTIAN

The drive back from small town Waikato hadn't been the smoothest Sebastian had ever driven. Roadworks on the highways had slowed him down, and made him irritable. His phone cord was wearing out, and his phone wasn't charging as quickly as he was accustomed to.

Finally, when he'd pulled into Auckland, he'd hit at peak time for rush hour traffic on the Southern Motorway.

Parking in the driveway of the ramshackle Mt Eden cottage he shared with Basil felt hard-won. He could barely register his relief — all he wanted was to get out of the car.

He retrieved his bags, and trudged to the house, ill-charged phone in hand.

Basil pounced immediately, even before Sebastian had removed his shoes, startling him into dropping a bag. Thankfully it was the bag with his clothes in it, not the one with his camera gear.

"There's mail for you! And it looks important."

Basil thrust a fancy envelope into Sebastian's hand. "Oh." Sebastian blinked at it. "Okay. Yes, hi."

"Oh! Sorry. Welcome home darling," Basil had the good grace to look embarrassed when he leaned in to kiss his cheek. "It's good to see you. Come in, sit down."

Basil took Sebastian's other bag and closed the door behind him, ushering him gently but firmly into the lounge. "How was your trip?"

Basil was obviously trying very hard, but his eyes kept flicking back to the envelope in Sebastian's hand. Sebastian decided he could tease him a little longer.

"It was all right, I didn't catch much on camera, but probably enough for a short episode. The place had a really storied history, I think you'd like to hear some of it."

Basil nodded, but his eyes were still on Sebastian's hand.

He turned the envelope over. Noting the lack of return address or postage stamp.

"It was hand-delivered while I was at work," Basil supplied.

Sebastian examined the writing on the front of the envelope, wondering. The envelope was sealed with a dramatic-looking red wax seal, and Sebastian wasn't sure how to open it without shattering the wax.

"There's a letter opener on the coffee table,"

Sebastian fixed Basil with a look. "Yes, of course. A completely ordinary thing to have out, Baz."

Basil blushed and adjusted his glasses.

Sebastian smiled, letting Basil know he was off the hook, and picked up the opener. It was old, antique probably, carved of bone. Sebastian slipped it under the seal and levered the linen envelope open. Inside was a single piece of heavy paper, almost cardstock. The words were stamped into it, rather than written. The author must have used an old-fashioned typewriter.

To Mssr. Sebastian Black, You are cordially invited to a retreat at Beach House commencing on February 29th Beginning with afternoon tea on the 29th, and ending after three nights.

The house is haunted, and it is my fondest hope that you and your esteemed partner Basil Harrison can assist with the troubles I have been experiencing. There will be several other experts in the supernatural in attendance. All meals, drinks, and comforts will be provided.

No need to RSVP, simply arrive at the address below before three in the afternoon of the 29th.

Yours,

Horatio

Sebastian was going to read it aloud, but Basil had sprung to his feet and moved behind Sebastian's chair to read over his shoulder. Sebastian held the letter still for him.

"A haunted house party invitation?" Basil mused.

Sebastian nodded. "Sounds like the start of a horror movie."

"Or an Agatha Christie novel."

"Either way the kind of set up where people die, right?" Sebastian folded the letter and slid it back into the envelope.

"Well, are we going to do it?"

"I don't know, Basil. I'm tired and cranky, I can't make a decision right now." Sebastian rubbed the bridge of his nose.

"Dinner. I've got dinner ready, I'll heat it up. You stay put." Basil squeezed his shoulder and left the room.

Sebastian peeled off his socks and stretched his legs.

Above him, the ceiling creaked in a familiar sort of way. "Hi Eek! Yes, I'm back."

"Good." The sound was so faint Sebastian could almost fool himself he hadn't heard it, but he had, and he took comfort in it.

They didn't have a pet, but their house monster offered a similar sort of comfort. Someone else who would notice when he was gone, and be glad he'd returned.

Sebastian pulled the letter out again, read it, and put it back in its envelope set it down on the coffee table once more. It was too good an opportunity to pass up, he knew that. But he dearly wanted to.

The ghosts didn't scare him, not really, he was used to ghosts now.

But the invitation mentioned other experts. What if Asher was there? The evil mage who had turned Sebastian into a cat for no reason than to mess with Basil? And then tried to kill them both as well as a bunch of innocent people. He had been defeated in his goal of sucking Basil's magic out of him, but he had also escaped. Disappeared via lightning. The most over the top dramatic villain exit Sebastian had ever seen.

If he looked like himself, they'd recognise him of course, but who's to say a powerful person like Asher couldn't disguise himself magically? It wouldn't surprise Sebastian at all if he was more akin to a hermit crab, changing shells whenever it suited him.

It was unlikely, a million to one chance that Asher would get an invite. He didn't have a public persona the way Sebastian did, after all. But that didn't stop the fear worrying at him, spiralling the 'what ifs' in his brain.

The other witches in Basil's local circle were nice, and he liked Basil's parents fine, but unknown witches and mages? There was no predicting what their magic could do. He'd feel like a rabbit surrounded by hunters and dogs. There was every chance he'd be in no danger, but the danger would still be close at hand.

Still, it would make a great series of episodes for his show.

And if he had any chance of getting past his fear of magic, which he did want to work through, he would have to do things like this. Put himself in uncomfortable situations. Magic was a part of his life, because he lived with a witch and a monster, and he couldn't imagine ever wanting to leave

Basil. Basil wasn't ever going to just stop having magic, he was always going to be, and attract, magic.

The same could be said of Sebastian, unless he quit his show and found a new career. He guessed there weren't a lot of jobs open to ex-YouTube ghost hunters, but maybe he could film sports or something. The idea of getting up early in winter to stand in a muddy field and film rugby players wasn't *entirely* without its attractions, but he knew he'd never be able to stick to something like that.

He loved his show. He loved investigating, meeting new people and learning the history of the places he visited. It was his life's passion.

Which meant he had to do what the old Sebastian would have done. Which was enthusiastically RSVP yes, pack his bags and hit the road.

Thankfully the dates were a week away, he did have some time to rest and cut together the Waikato footage.

Basil set a dinner tray on Sebastian's lap. His eyes flicked to the envelope on the table. He was practically vibrating with holding back the question.

"Can you get some time off work, or swap shifts for next week?"

Basil clapped his hands and bounced on his heels. Adorable. "Yes! I'm still owed annual leave, I was terrible at taking it before I met you."

"Then I guess we're heading into an Agatha Christie novel." Sebastian grinned as Basil kissed his forehead.

"Wonderful!"

Basil's excitement was infectious. He'd made the right choice. Anything that made Basil that happy was the right choice.

"We'll have to position ourselves as the Poirot or the Miss Marple characters," Sebastian said, smiling lazily. "Then we can be sure of coming out of this terrible situation unscathed."

"You sound like Hercule already." Basil sat beside him and caught him up on the news of the library and the Mt Eden witch's coven, as Sebastian tucked into his meal.

CHAPTER THREE

BASIL

The week passed slowly. Basil had no trouble booking time off, and finding cover for the shifts he was missing. He was getting used to leaving the library to the other staff, and rather enjoying the time off as well.

He packed and repacked his bags, ensuring he had packed some fancy clothing options, envisioning a grand ball, or dinner parties with dress requirements, alongside his usual daywear. Of course, he also packed his favourite books of magic, his grimoire, a collection of crystals and dried herbs from his garden, his deck of tarot cards, and a few other magical odds and ends, just in case.

Finally, the day came, they packed up Sebastian's car and drove out. It wasn't too much of a trek, a while past Warkworth on the North Shore. Not quite an hour to go over the harbour bridge and navigate the traffic.

As he drove, Sebastian's nerves seemed to be easing. Basil knew he liked the view of the city from the bridge, so snapped a couple of photos on his phone to show him later.

It was a clear day, and Auckland city, arranged at the base of a volcano, with the peaks of more volcanoes visible all around, was kind of a strange thing to be comforted by. That casual threat of possible destruction always there, but Basil was soothed all the same. It was his city. Out towards the east, Rangitoto and past it, Waiheke Island, where Basil had grown up.

They weren't even leaving the city, not really, but the further north they drove, the more it felt like a holiday.

Basil had made a playlist on Sebastian's Spotify account and was pleased when Sebastian started to sing along with it. It was a positive sign.

Sebastian turned off the main highways, following the map on his phone through Warkworth proper and towards the coast. He pulled them into a long driveway. Twenty metres in there was a forbidding brick and iron gate, which stood open, guarded by two stone lions. The gate stood open.

Basil's stomach tensed and he felt a slight frisson of tension in the air. This wasn't just an ordinary gate, and whatever lay beyond... he hoped he was strong enough to face up to it.

Sebastian

The lightness Sebastian had been feeling from the drive faded as he turned onto the gravel driveway. It was beautiful, with arcing oaks lining the road, and the gorgeous old gate, but something felt ... off about it all.

"Isn't it so impressive, Bastian?" Basil asked, but even his tone didn't sound thrilled.

Sebastian took the driveway slowly. When he pulled into the wide turning circle and Sebastian paused to take a look at the house, he was slightly disappointed.

He couldn't help but compare this to their first sighting of the Waitomo Hotel. That had been large, impressive, eerie to look at with darkened windows and a deeply unsettling aura to it. Beach House looked like a really well kept up colonial villa. One that had probably been made into a Bed and Breakfast.

The white painted weatherboards were bright and fresh, the grounds looked tidy, immaculately kept, and there were warm glowing lights in all the windows.

His initial disappointment was replaced with relief. If the place looked like this, perhaps there was nothing much to fear here? Just a homeowner with delusions of being the next Alastair Crowley? Holding seances for fun?

Sebastian pulled the car in next to another one in what seemed to be the parking area.

"Looks like a nice place to have a few relaxing days," he said.

"Mm."

Sebastian knew the tone of that 'mm', and he didn't like it one bit.

Basil stared at the building as if it had personally insulted his parents, his eyes narrowed, his mouth in a sharp frown.

"You sense something?" Sebastian asked, mouth dry.

Basil nodded, and Sebastian's heart sank. "There's, well, an aura to it. It's not necessarily ghosts, but it could well be."

Basil didn't move, even to undo his seatbelt. Sebastian, without knowing it, had removed his seatbelt, opened the car door and had one foot out.

Cold sweat dripped down his back. "Should we go? We could turn around and head straight back home?"

"No, I —" Basil swallowed audibly. "It's, I think I can help here."

Sebastian's stomach knotted. Between the dry mouth, the sweat and now the pain in his gut he felt like he was about to be sick, or that he was coming down with a terrible 'flu.

Well. He'd wanted this — a solid episode for SpectreWatch. Maybe it would even be healing, facing his fears and all that.

All the same he offered up a silent prayer for protection from his ancestors, and Papatuanuku, the earth mother.

"We should go in," Basil sounded much more determined now. "We can help. I know it."

"Gotcha."

They unpacked the car.

The front door to the house opened and a person with a purple-dyed quiff came out to watch them. They looked youngish, maybe late twenties, and wore a shirt with a pattern of dinosaurs on it, along with baggy acid-washed jeans.

"Good afternoon," Sebastian called out.

The person waved and came down the stairs to greet them.

"Is it okay to leave the car here?" Sebastian gestured. He'd added his car to a line, but it was always polite to check.

"Totally fine. I'm Horatio, I'm your host this weekend. Thank you for coming." They offered a hand to shake.

Sebastian took it. "Pleased to meet you. I'm Sebastian Black and this is Basil Harrison."

"A pleasure. You're both he/hims, right? My pronouns are they/them."

"Yes, hes and hims."

Basil came around to shake Horatio's hand as well.

"I hope your drive wasn't too awful."

"No, it was very smooth," Sebastian said.

"Can I help with your luggage?"

"Well, you could take this one, thank you," Basil handed over a tote bag Sebastian couldn't remember seeing being loaded into the car.

Sebastian shouldered his things and they went up the stairs and through the doors of Beach House.

The moment he stepped through the door the temperature dropped significantly. Once he crossed the threshold the cold eased, as if it was just the zone around the door that was chilly.

The house was dim inside, despite the cheery lights he'd seen from outside. Perhaps they were too low a wattage?

The foyer smelled pleasantly of beeswax floor polish and something roasting. Sebastian's stomach rumbled.

Horatio heard it, and laughed over their shoulder. "Dinner will be in about an hour, but if you're peckish there's finger food out in the parlour. A lot of the guests are already here, settling in, but a few might be in there. Come on, you're up here, follow me."

Horatio lead the way up the carpeted stairs.

CHAPTER FOUR

BASIL

Walking through the door and into Beach House felt like being doused in ice-cold water. Basil shuddered bodily, and stopped walking. Sebastian and Horatio didn't seem to notice anything strange.

He had sensed ancient wards somewhere on the door. He made a mental note to investigate those later. They felt eroded, twisted almost. He'd read that could happen with wards left too long without maintenance.

He didn't want to let Sebastian out of his sight so he hurried to keep up, he was talking to Horatio but Basil was too distracted to make out what they were saying.

The name Beach House evoked a small bach, something made in the 1950s or 60s perhaps, with an old surfboard out the front and a rope strung between porch posts for a washing line. It would be situated on a scrubby, sandy grass lawn and across a worn road from the beach.

But Beach House was none of those things, except relatively close to the water.

But it wasn't the look of the place that unsettled Basil, not really. He had a sensation crawling up his back. The house itself seemed to be watching them. Added to that — a kind of anticipation. The feeling of someone holding their breath, or perhaps the quiet in a symphony hall after the conductor has taken their place, but before the orchestra begins to play.

Maybe I should have listened to Sebastian, and we should drive away. I don't like this sensation one bit.

"Your rooms are here. There's an attached bathroom, so you don't have to share with anyone." Horatio pushed a door open. There was an antique ceramic plaque on the door that read *The Blue Room*. Inside, all the walls were papered with blue wallpaper. It was an old-fashioned paper, with a design of ornate repeating diamonds.

The room was larger than Basil had expected, with a generously sized bed on a heavy wooden frame, sporting a blue patchwork quilt.

Sebastian set the bags down beside a vast wooden desk and opened the curtains.

The sensation of being watched had eased somewhat since walking into the bedroom. *I'll need to cleanse the room thoroughly though, check there's no malevolent spirits present.*

"Here's your key to the room," Horatio handed Basil a keychain with an old fashioned oval shaped tag on it. "There are fresh towels, toiletries and so on in the bathroom cupboard and there's a kettle and tea things on the table by the wardrobe. As I said there's finger food downstairs right now and —"

Horatio was cut off by the insistent beeping of a car horn in the driveway. "Ah, that'll be the next guests. I'd better go meet them. See you at dinner, six sharp."

Horatio bustled off, removing a lot of agitated energy from the room.

Basil closed the door behind them and breathed out heavily. He placed his hand on the wood of the door, just under the ancient-looking brass coat hooks, and his magic welled inside him instantly. The purple light coming readily to imprint a charm of protection into the door. Something that would prevent anyone entering who meant Sebastian or him harm.

The charm glowed under his hand, a twisting rune, then vanished, sinking into the old oak.

"You um, did that fast," Sebastian said.

Basil turned to reassure his boyfriend. "This house, I don't know but there's something watchful about it. I wanted us to have a safe space."

"Even I can feel something." Sebastian rubbed his own arm, looking around the room as if searching. "It's a classic haunted house, isn't it? Straight out of a movie."

Basil went to his suitcase and opened it, rifling through for the bag of crystals he'd packed. "I'll give you some of these to keep in your pocket while we're here."

Sebastian moved to look out the window. "Whoever it is who just arrived, they look like — I don't know. Like if this house was in a sixties horror film they'd be the main characters."

"I suppose they're other experts, but what?" Basil found what he wanted and moved beside Sebastian, touching his shoulder with his. "A demonologist? A priest? Who would you invite?"

"Every exorcist I could find?" Sebastian's eyes watched the new couple.

A man and a woman. He was dressed all in black with a black cowboy hat, she looked like she'd been dressed by Laura Ashley.

"Let's hope dinner isn't pea soup, eh?" He nudged Sebastian gently, trying to make him laugh.

"Gross." Sebastian leaned his head on Basil's shoulder and sighed.

Basil hugged him with one arm and slipped the crystals into his pocket. "Keep those on you. We'll be all right whatever happens. We always are."

Sebastian straightened up and gave Basil a brave smile. "Yeah. Unstoppable team, right?"

"Unstoppable."

CHAPTER FIVE

SEBASTIAN

S ebastian led the way to the parlour. There were trays of cheese, crackers, grapes, and fruit spreads on the sideboard. The room was cheerful, with a crackling fire and the heavy drapes pulled open. Overstuffed armchairs sat here and there, and if it were another house, Sebastian could easily imagine spending hours there, reading or napping.

The two new arrivals were already inside the room. Sebastian guessed they were in their sixties, possibly older. The man was white, with grey hair and smile lines around his blue eyes. He wore a black jacket and shirt, a Western string tie fastened with a tiny skull, and black jeans. He had black cowboy boots on but apparently had left the hat off. The woman was dressed in a peach calf-length floral skirt, a sleeveless beige shell top, and peach cardigan over her shoulders. Her hair was slate grey, bobbed at her jawbone.

They both lit up with bright smiles when Basil and Sebastian walked in.

"Well, howdy there!" the man strode forward, hand extended. "I'm Randall Rhodes, and this here's my wife, Laura-May. She's a medium with some psychic powers."

Sebastian shook Randall's hand, his grip was crushing. "Pleased to meet you. I'm Sebastian and this is my boyfriend Basil, he's a witch. I film things for my documentary show."

Laura-Mae shook Sebastian's hand in a more genteel manner as Randall moved on to Basil.

"You're reducing yourself to 'I film things'?" Basil exclaimed. "You're an expert at researching local history, cryptids, and folklore, and you know how to work a thousand different technical contraptions."

Sebastian ducked his head. "Thanks Basil."

"A witch eh? Well it sure is a pleasure to meet you both. Don't often come across male witches, do we Randy?" Laura-Mae's accent wasn't as thick as her husband's. The two of them shared a laugh.

Sebastian swallowed a laugh, not at their apparent joke but at how over the top they were. *Are these two for real?*

The door to the hallway slammed shut, causing all four of them to jump.

"Oh Goddess," Basil breathed.

"Bless my heart!" Laura-Mae said in the same moment.

"Is that the kind of activity Horatio was referring to in the invite, do you think?" Sebastian asked Basil.

"Oh certainly," Laura-Mae answered. "It's happened three times since we arrived. The spirits are very restless."

Sebastian realised Basil had taken his arm rather tightly. "Okay?"

Basil's face was paler than before but he nodded. "Yes. Just, thought of Asher," he murmured, not quite quiet enough for the Rhodeses not to hear. "Who's Asher?" Randall asked.

"No one. Old acquaintance," Sebastian said.

"Is he expected at this house party?" Laura-Mae asked, her expression bland but her eyes flicking between the two of them.

"No," Basil said.

"He's dead, or...indisposed." Sebastian added.

"I think we will hear from many of the dead," Laura-Mae intoned. She'd dropped the tone of her voice an octave and her expression became suddenly grave.

"We'll see, won't we?" The door opened and a young woman with straight brown hair walked in. Her glasses were large, the frames taking up most of her small featured face. She was dressed in a blue T-shirt with a picture of a frog on the breast, and worn-in jeans.

Sebastian offered to shake with the newcomer. "Hi there, I'm Sebastian and this is my boyfriend Basil, and the Rhodes."

"Brit Stevenson." The woman shook his hand briefly and gave a tight smile to the others. "I'm a theoretical physicist."

"Sounds intriguing," Basil said. "I'm a librarian, and well, a witch."

"Of course you are," Brit's smile became more strained. "And you two are...?" She turned to Laura-Mae and Randall as if expecting the worst.

"A medium and a demonologist," Randall said, pointing to his wife and then hooking his thumb at his own chest.

Sebastian had to suppress a laugh, after all Basil had guessed correctly.

Randall cleared his throat at Brit's unimpressed expression. "I'm guessin' you're the resident skeptic, then?"

"You'd be quite correct." Brit helped herself to some cheese and crackers. "I'm sure it will be a fun few days for all of us. I, for one, intend to eat a lot, and catch up on my reading. There's an extensive library, apparently."

"There is?" Basil perked all the way up. "How wonderful."

Sebastian took a salmon puff from the side of the charcuterie board. It was delicious. Brit's approach might be a stroke of genius.

But his gut reminded him by sinking dramatically — Basil was certain this house was haunted, and Horatio had asked for their help.

He did want to help.

The door to the parlour shut itself again.

"There, you see?" Randall widened his eyes at Brit.

"Probably just poorly hung," Brit said.

Sebastian licked the remains of salmon mousse from his lips. He could eat *and* work. Horatio seemed pretty up front and decent, perhaps the problem could be solved quite quickly and Sebastian would be able to focus on the food?

As if summoned, Horatio opened the door and ushered in a tall, blonde person wearing overalls decorated with a pattern of brightly coloured mushrooms. Their flowing hair was held back by a daisy hair clip on one side and their facial hair was artfully trimmed. Small tattoos covered their bare arms, with a number on their hands and fingers, some Sebastian thought could be runes.

The two of them were laughing about something, like old friends.

Sebastian hadn't heard another car in the driveway, but then they'd been talking.

Horatio saw all their eyes on them and smiled. "This is almost all of the guests now. I've had word that some are running late. Everyone, this is Kris Crimson, they/she pronouns."

Kris raised their hand. "Hi all."

"Another medium, I can sense it," Laura-Mae surged forward, her arms outstretched to clasp Kris's hands in her own. "I can already tell we'll get along like a mama cat and its kit."

Kris smiled in a lop-sided way. "Uh, thanks, but I'm a mage."

"A mage?" Sebastian whispered to Basil. "Like Asher was?"

Basil shivered. "Let's hope not."

Horatio was listing off names for Kris's benefit.

"Just before we go into dinner, I have some staff on this weekend I'd like you to meet."

Horatio went to the side door and called out, four people soon came filing in.

"This is Mindy, she's in charge of cleaning your rooms but she'll only be here for a few hours every second day, so please take charge of keeping things neat yourself. Eve is our chef de cuisine, if you have any allergies or intolerances around food, please see her. Finally, Andrew here is an all-rounder, helping in the kitchen, doing yard work. Generally keeping the whole place running. They'll all be off-duty after dinner, but feel free to approach them during the day if you need anything."

Horatio turned and rattled off the names of the guests for the staff's benefit.

Everyone greeted each other with 'hello's and 'kia ora's although the looks exchanged were somewhat guarded, as if the staff suspected the guests of wanting to trick them, and the guests were thinking the same thing about the staff.

Eve cleared her throat to break the stretching silence. "Please, come through to the dining room, dinner will be served once you're all seated."

They filed into the dining room and found name cards at each place setting around the large rectangular table.

"For the first night I thought I'd give you set places," Horatio said. "No need to stick to them after tonight, I thought it might be nice for you all not to have to make decisions while you're settling in."

Sebastian and Basil's places were side by side, next to Laura-Mae and Randall. The other side of the table had Brit, Kris and two empty seats. Horatio took the head of the table.

"I'm the only scientist here, am I?" Brit asked. Sebastian thought he detected a trace of Australian in her accent.

"That's right," Horatio answered. "We have a witch, a ghost hunter, a demonologist, a medium, a mage and later this evening a pair of occult specialists are expected. I asked some Catholic priests, Shinto priests, Buddhist monks, and even a shaman but none of them replied. I also went to the elders of the local Marae but they said they'd come by after you've all left."

"To mop up the mess?" Brit smirked.

"Sounds very pragmatic of the elders," Sebastian said.

Horatio shrugged. "It'll be interesting to see what they say, and what all of you come up with in the next few days."

The food was served family style, with large bowls of salads, beef stew, vegetarian risotto, fresh sliced bread and chicken drumsticks. It all smelled incredible, and Sebastian's stomach rumbled its impatience. He was starved.

Sebastian piled his plate with a little bit of everything, sending silent apologies and thanks to the spirits of the animals who had perished for their meal. Beside him Basil was doing the same thing.

"Before we eat, I'd like to say grace," Laura-Mae said.

Brit rolled her eyes. "How about you say it to yourself."

"Now then, we're all here for the same reason, let's be civil," Laura-Mae smiled, shaking her head at the scientist. "Thank you lord, for the food in front of us, we ask that we be blessed this evening, and stay protected from any demons or ill-natured spirits that might be sharing the roof with us. In the name of the father, the son, and the holy spirit, amen."

While she spoke, Sebastian dropped his head in respect, but Basil simply sighed. Brit started eating, and when Sebastian looked up after, Horatio and Kris looked distinctly unimpressed.

"Nice Grace, Laura-Mae," Randall said, beaming at her proudly. "Isn't she a peach?"

"Indeed," Basil said, drily.

The meal distracted everyone from talking about anything besides how tasty it was, and asking for this plate or that to be passed.

Once everyone was tucking in, the household staff joined them, sitting at the far end of the table from Horatio. Sebastian was quietly thrilled that it wasn't some kind of elitist upstairs/downstairs kind of situation.

When people had finished, Eve and Andrew cleared away the dishes. Horatio clasped their hands together on the table and looked between them all.

"As far as rules for the long weekend go, you have free run of the house and gardens, except of course, occupied bedrooms. Those are off-limits for obvious reasons. The attic isn't very sound so please don't go up there either. The cellar is fine though, and can be accessed via the kitchen. Please don't hang about the kitchen if the staff are trying to work though, we all want to be fed."

There was a round of gentle laughter around the table.

"The house is a bit of a cell service dead zone," Horatio continued. "There are a few places you might be able to get a bar or two, I usually use the gazebo on the West lawn. There are drinks and snacks available at all times from the kitchen. If you need anything special please find me or one of the staff."

"Thank you," Basil said. "So, for clarity's sake, you want us to put the spirits to rest, is that right?"

"Yes. There have been a lot of disturbances and I'd like them to stop. I really want a regular country house, not one full of spirits."

"Have you had a building inspector through?" Brit asked. "That door keeps slamming shut and I'm sure it's poorly installed. Incorrectly hung doors can behave that way."

"Yes, several. Plus Andrew's checked over everything and he's our handyman."

"Mm." Brit didn't look at all convinced."

"So, yes, do what you like, start investigations tonight or tomorrow. I'm truly grateful to you all for coming."

"If I could just ask…" Sebastian raised his hand and immediately put it down again.

"Ask anything you like." Horatio nodded.

"What have you seen in this place that has you worried? I mean, aside from the slamming doors."

There was a murmur around the table as if everyone had been waiting for this question to be asked.

"Cold patches, weird noises at night," Horatio paused and ran a hand through their short hair. "I've heard knocking on the walls quite a few times."

"The house settling, most likely. Drafts too, it's an old house" Brit said.

"Perhaps. Strong draft to turn the key in my bedroom door and operate the doorknob."

Laura-Mae laughed, a touch of derision in it. "Before this weekend is up, you'll be singing a different tune, Miss Scientist."

"It's Mx Scientist, actually," Brit said. "I'm non-binary, I don't mind she/her pronouns."

"Knocking sounds frightening," Kris leaned forward, focused on Horatio. "Does it make a pattern of knocks or is it more random?"

"Insistent." Horatio frowned. "Soft knocking to begin with, like someone is asking to enter, then it gets louder, and goes on longer. It's very much like a person knocking to get in."

Kris grimaced. "Horrible."

Horatio nodded.

"Right, so I'm going to go and sit by the fire —"

There was a resounding bang from the front of the house.

Sebastian startled, one hand grabbing for Basil.

Kris yelped.

"The door." Horatio stood, then sat down again. The others looked ruffled.

In a moment Andrew opened the dining room door and two impressive-looking people strode in. The man was in a full charcoal grey suit, his mid-brown skin clear and glowing under carefully groomed black hair. The woman wore a striking geometric patterned dress with one huge shoulder piece. It looked like something from a Parisian fashion show. She had deep red hair, half pinned up, and skin so pale it was almost translucent.

"Good evening all," the man said, in a deep and cheerful voice. "I'm Francois, and this fine lady is my better half." Francois turned to take his wife's hand. "The light of my existence, my absolute hero."

"Oh Francois." The woman beamed, ducking her head.

"Wendla, is her name." He managed to say it before she surged in to kiss him full on the mouth.

The two kissed for a few long seconds, then turned to beam at everyone seated at the table, Wendla with her arm through Francois's as if it were second nature. "Bergman, we're the Bergmans," Wendla said.

Sebastian loved them instantly. They were larger than life, like something from a glamorous old Hollywood movie.

"I'm Sebastian," he said, reaching over the table to shake their hands.

"Charmed," Wendla shook his hand firmly and flashed Sebastian a warm smile.

"Please, sit," Horatio said. "Are you hungry? I'm sure there's plenty of leftovers."

"Oh I couldn't eat a thing," Francois said.

"I'll take a look later," Wendla said, sitting as Francois pulled a chair for her. "Thank you, doll."

"Sorry, just one more question from me," Sebastian said. "I have a YouTube channel, documentary style reporting on ghost hunts and investigations. Please let me know, all of you, if you're all right being included in the footage or if you'd rather not. I have release forms, you can sign them if you're willing to be on camera."

"Of course, darling," Wendla said.

The other guests nodded.

"I'm happy to," Kris said. "But sometimes tech and me don't get along. So, uh, be warned? If something expensive shorts out I probably can't afford to replace it."

Sebastian chuckled. "Maybe no super close camera work?"

Horatio shook their head. "If you don't mind I'd rather not be on camera, it's a privacy thing."

"I understand," Sebastian said. "I'd also be happy to show you the episode before I release it. It's your house, you should have the final say."

"I appreciate that. I don't mind if you film me in the background, and you can use footage where I'm talking, I'd rather not have a clear image of me associated with this house being out on the internet."

Sebastian nodded. "Of course, that's very doable."

"Now, if you don't mind, I'm going to go and read. If anyone has questions, I'll be through here." Horatio got up and walked towards the parlour.

Laura-Mae leaned towards Sebastian. "I expect you'll be wanting to do interviews with all of us? We're free right now if you'd like to get started."

Sebastian hadn't thought too much further than establishing shots and filming searches of the rooms, but it seemed like a fine idea, and definitely good material. He was sure his viewers would enjoy having a proper intro to the weekend's cast of characters.

"Yeah, great, let's do it. Why don't you find a suitable spot and I'll grab my gear?"

CHAPTER SIX

BASIL

Watching Sebastian interview Laura-Mae and Randall set Basil's teeth on edge. Like he was listening to all three of them drag their nails down a blackboard.

Laura-Mae and Randall had found a grand-looking living room and were seated in front of a large oil portrait of an austere-looking gentleman. Looking at the display panel of Sebastian's camera, it framed them very dramatically.

Basil didn't like to jump to conclusions about people, but of everyone he'd met, these two struck him as disingenuous. He wouldn't go so far as to call them charlatans or liars, not yet at any rate, but something about them felt like a veneer.

Sebastian, however, was a consummate professional. He smiled, and leaned an elbow on the armchair and asked his questions with genuine interest. "Can you tell me what you were doing when you got the invitation to Beach House?"

"Well," Laura-Mae said. "I was in the middle of communing with the spirits. Automatic writing, you know. I'm always so attuned to what they have to say, when I was struck with gosh-darned certainty that some important message had arrived."

Basil ducked behind the camera in order to roll his eyes undetected.

"Obviously, she couldn't just stop," Randall said. "So I went to check the mail."

"How did you know what she'd sensed?" Sebastian asked, gently.

"Oh, she told me."

There was a pause.

Basil had never been a medium, but he'd met a few with Sebastian over the last ten months, chasing paranormal phenomena. When automatic writing was happening, the medium was usually in a trance, or meditative flow, focused entirely on listening and writing. He wasn't sure he'd ever see one multi-task to the degree that they could turn to their partner and ask them to do a chore. Still, maybe she was gifted?

"And that's when you received the invite?"

"Correct."

"And you're both from the United States, isn't that right?"

"Yes, Sir." Randall said. "But we moved to New Zealand recently, so I guess Horatio had been tracking us so to speak. The invite found us in Tauranga."

"And, Laura-Mae, when did you first discover your gifts?" Sebastian pressed on.

Laura-Mae smiled wide. "When I was fifteen. I've always assumed it was tied to my maturing body. Something happens to a girl when she becomes a woman. I was a late bloomer, and I believe it was because of my gift. I was asleep in bed one night, and something woke me up. I opened my eyes to see an apparition, a glowing white woman standing over me. I knew, as certain as I know I have two hands, that it was my maternal great-grandmother. She was letting me know my powers had awakened."

"That sounds lovely," Sebastian said. "Did she speak to you?"

"Oh yes, she told me about a necklace she'd hidden in the eaves of the old family barn." Laura-May had pulled a silver cross out and was holding it one hand.

"Was the necklace there when you went to look for it?" Sebastian asked.

Laura-Mae frowned and her grip on the cross tightened. Her expression remained bright but something flickered in her eyes. "I'm not sure. I didn't get a chance to visit it properly before I sold it, when I was twenty-one. But my great-grandmother wouldn't have lied, not about that."

"We have tried to get in touch with the current owners about access," Randall said. His down-home bonhomie was wearing a bit thin.

Laura-Mae continued. "They've been less than helpful."

"Friendly as a coyote with a cactus in its paw." Randall nodded.

"You know how it is." Laura-Mae leaned closer in, dropping her voice slightly and taking his hand like she was planning to faith heal him. "So many poor, uneducated souls say we're liars or con-artists. It's the easiest thing for them to say, the quickest conclusion. It's unfair but people like us have to be patient."

Sebastian hesitated, his eyebrows drawing together. "People like us?"

Basil didn't dare breathe. Sure, Sebastian had money, and worked for himself, but he was also Māori, and the Māori as a people were still feeling the effects of centuries of discrimination. Laura-Mae didn't seem to understand the implications of what she was saying.

"Those sensitive to the spiritual realm. So many are quick to judge. They're simply coming from a place of ignorance and fear. They have never opened their third eye to look beyond the veil."

"Mm." Sebastian's mouth formed a flat line. He directed his attention to Randall. "And you, can you tell us about your gifts?"

"I've always been aware of things that others couldn't see. Strange shadows, shapes in the dark, you know. I made it my life's purpose to read everything I could about myths, folklore and so on. I studied everything I could, now I'm number one in the world for my knowledge of demons and other monsters."

Basil raised an eyebrow. *Someone was ranking who knew the most about demons? That sounded entirely fabricated.*

"I'm sure you are." There was a tension in Sebastian's jaw now. Basil could see it was only a matter of moments before he entirely lost his patience. "Randall met Big Foot, you know," Laura-Mae said.

Basil noted with alarm that she had settled back into the chair and looked as if she could talk for hours. He had to intervene and rescue Sebastian. "Perhaps we should wrap it up there," he said. "It's properly dark outside now and I know Sebastian wanted to take some establishing shots of the place, in the dark."

Laura-Mae looked surprised but could hardly argue. "Well, of course. If you need more interviews with us we're in the Bird Room. Of course I'll share your little show with my many thousands of viewers, in exchange for a favourable portrayal."

"I will of course, appreciate the exposure," Sebastian sounded positively strangled now.

Basil shut off the camera and stepped forward. "Thank you so much for your time."

Sebastian busied himself packing away the filming gear as Basil ushered Laura-Mae and Randall out of the room.

He closed the door behind them and counted to thirty.

Then he caught Sebastian's eye. They managed to hold out a few seconds before bursting into gales of laughter.

"He met Big Foot?" Basil sputtered. "I wonder if they shook hands?" Sebastian giggled.

"He was probably waiting for us to ask if we could see the photo of them together."

Sebastian slapped his back and the two of them struggled to breathe.

"We shouldn't judge," Sebastian said finally. "We have a brightly coloured monster living in our house."

"Yes, that's true." Basil rubbed his aching side. "And besides, judging probably means we're poorly educated and ignorant."

Sebastian nodded solemnly. "We shouldn't doubt the world's number one demonologist."

***

It took a while for the laughter to truly die down.

"Let's get a little filming done tonight in the halls," Sebastian said. He was changing out the memory card from the camera for a fresh one. "See if we can pick up anything?"

Basil nodded, then yawned. "Not for too long though, I feel as if we've already been here for days, not hours."

Sebastian nodded, and packed away everything but his small handheld camera. "Let's see what this haunted mansion has for us."

They walked the halls for a while. No one else was out, everyone seemed to have turned in for the night. That was something of a relief to Basil. The shots of the long, empty halls would look good on camera, and Sebastian's nervousness didn't need to be tested by mages and psychics.

Beach House's hallways were curiously extensive. There seemed too many of them for the size of the house, but Basil kept this observation to himself.

As they walked, instead, he tuned in to his second sight, and tried to detect something of the presence he'd felt when they'd first arrived.

Nothing ... it was an old house, and he felt a strange vibe for sure, but nothing pinged at him or seized him like when he'd walked over the threshold.

After a half hour, Sebastian led them back to their room. "May as well get some rest," Sebastian said. "The stuff I got tonight will be good for atmosphere if nothing else, but I'll play it back carefully and check for sounds... when we're back home."

Basil nodded. Often on a hunt like this, Sebastian would stay up all night reviewing footage or trying to get more. One more sign he wasn't himself.

They got ready for bed, Basil unable to stop himself yawning again and again. The drive must have taken more out of him than he'd thought.

He snuggled up to Sebastian, tucking under his arm and slinging his own over his boyfriend's chest. "I love you."

"Love you too." Sebastian kissed Basil's forehead and switched off the lights. Basil fell asleep instantly.

CHAPTER SEVEN

SEBASTIAN

S ebastian was surprised when Basil slept so fast, but sometimes situations like this took it out of his magical boyfriend. Something about the effort it took subconsciously to keep evil spirits at bay... Basil was good at protection magic, that was how he'd first 'come out' about being magical to Sebastian after all. That glowing purple shield back at the library.

It seemed so long ago now.

Sebastian looked around the room, which was far darker than their bedroom at home. No street lights outside to filter in. Instead they had heavy curtains and the weight of history.

He didn't feel entirely comfortable in the room, but Basil's weight, pressed against him, was soothing enough that he eventually dropped off.

Sebastian had no idea how many hours later it was that Basil struck him across the jaw, but it was still pitch black in their room.

Sebastian flinched back from him, tangled in the blankets and unable to create space. Basil thrashed, like he was fighting some invisible foe.

Basil was also breathing way too fast.

Basil launched upwards, fighting the blankets now too, gasping like he couldn't get enough air. His eyes were screwed closed.

A dream? A vision?

Sebastian sat up and flicked on the light, but that didn't wake Basil.

He had to intervene though. He grabbed at Basil's shoulder. "Basil! Baz, wake up! It's a dream, it's only a dream." Sebastian hoped beyond hope that it *was* just a dream. He had no idea what he'd do if Basil didn't wake up.

Basil gripped his arm with both hands and heaved a breath like a man suffocating, but his eyes were still closed, and his lower body thrashed, kicking Sebastian in the shins. "Ow," Sebastian shook Basil a bit more vigorously, if he didn't wake him soon Sebastian would be black and blue in the morning. "Basil! Basil it's me, Sebastian. Wake up, now! Break free of whatever it is and look at me!"

Basil's eyes snapped open and his body went slack. He was panting like he'd run a marathon.

Sebastian rubbed his jaw, it smarted where Basil had hit him.

"You okay?"

Basil shook his head, his chest heaving as he took in air. "Thought I was drowning."

"A dream?" Sebastian switched to rubbing Basil's back, hoping it wasn't a sudden onset of asthma or something. "You're okay now."

It took a few minutes for Basil to get control of himself and his breathing, but finally he nodded his head, and turned to grab for a glass of water from the nightstand, which he sipped tentatively.

"You were dreaming," Sebastian said, at a loss.

"I was," Basil said. "But it also sort of ... I'm not sure. I was in this room, and I could see it all, I could see you and the curtains and everything, it was so real. Then, the room filled up with water, it was so fast, I couldn't see where it came from. I guess it was seeping up through the floorboards? And it swamped the bed, and then I couldn't breathe, I was trying to swim for the surface, and it was so dark, the water so dark and murky I couldn't see you..."

Tears trickled down Basil's cheeks, and Sebastian pulled him in to rest on his chest. He could feel Basil's heart still thudding where their chests touched.

"Took ages to wake you up," he murmured.

Basil nodded. "I think it was some kind of vision. It felt so real, so ..." he buried his head against Sebastian's pyjama top and sniffed.

"It's okay, it's over now," Sebastian didn't add 'I hope' although he was aware he had no way of knowing one way or another. He checked his watch. "It's almost six, that means the sun will be up soon, that's usually a good thing in terms of vindictive ghosts, right?"

Basil nodded, and sighed gently. "You smell so good. You smell of home." Sebastian couldn't help but smile, seeing Basil relax because of how Sebastian smelled. "We're each other's home. But... you could apologise for punching me."

Basil looked up, eyes bleary. "I what?"

"I woke up because you punched me." Sebastian turned his head so Basil could see his jaw. It smarted, so he was sure it'd be red. "See? Here."

"Oh goddess, I'm sorry," Basil laid a cool hand over Sebastian's jaw and the dull ache faded away. "I never thought I had it in me."

Sebastian had to laugh at that. "Neither to be honest. You kicked me too, but those don't hurt any more."

Basil shook his head and laughed as well. "I'm sorry. Maybe I'll sleep on the edge of the bed from now on?"

Sebastian pulled him in again, tightening his grip. "Don't you dare."

They went back to sleep like that, holding each other, with the light still on.

The sound of a gong woke them.

"I guess that means breakfast is served?" Basil muttered, sitting up and stretching out.

Sebastian swallowed, his mouth was dry as a desert and he hoped there'd be a good range of juices at breakfast. He had a hankering for a bubble tea, but there was far less hope of getting one of those all this way out of town.

They dressed and headed downstairs, Sebastian leaving his camera gear behind so he could focus on the meal.

Not everyone was up for breakfast. Horatio and Kris sat in the same spots they'd been in the night before, Laura-Mae and Randall had taken the next seats in at the grand table. There was no sign of Francois, Wendla or Brit.

Horatio looked up as they came in. They were wearing a loose mint green T-shirt with a cartoon of a happy rabbit on it and the slogan *How about no?* "Good morning, sleep well?"

"It wasn't exactly uneventful," Basil said. "Bit of a nightmare, but I did get back to sleep after it."

"Ah, I'm sorry to hear that," Horatio said. "The breakfast is set up buffet style on the sideboard, please help yourself."

"I daresay a nightmare in this place is indicative of demonic activity," Randall said. He was dressed in black again. Laura-Mae wore a pale pink twinset and pearls. She wiggled her fingers at Sebastian in a sort of wave. He nodded back, a little uncertain. Were they for real?

"Demonic? I thought it was far more likely to be uneasy spirits," Basil said. He was loading a plate with bacon, scrambled eggs, sausages and toast.

Sebastian decided on some of the bircher muesli and a croissant with cheese. The breakfast buffet was up there with a fine restaurant's breakfast offerings.

And yes, alongside urns of coffee and tea, there was a large basin of ice in which sat bottles of fresh juices. He grabbed two, a kiwifruit spirulina and an orange. He felt like he needed it. He set his things down beside Kris while Basil made himself the perfect cup of tea.

"How'd everyone else sleep?"

"Fine," Kris said. "But I felt stuff all night, disturbances, I guess. Maybe I felt it when Basil had his vision? I wish I'd brought my familiar with me, he'd help..."

Horatio frowned. "You could have, what kind of animal is your familiar?"

"A Leonberger," Kris said. "They're... very big dogs. He'd have knocked over everything in this dining room, just for a start. He's with friends this weekend, he'll be fine."

Horatio nodded. "Okay. Maybe... not."

Laura-Mae frowned deeply. She nudged Randall and he cleared his throat.

"You have a familiar, Kris?"

"Yes, did you want to see the picture?"

"Not at all." Randall shook his head, as if what he was about to say pained him. "But it's a very suspicious thing, a person with a familiar. Animals that talk or communicate, that's the work of the Devil."

"Randall," Horatio snapped. "Your beliefs are your beliefs, but I don't want to hear them over breakfast. None of the guests here are your enemies."

Kris flushed and shot Horatio a grateful look.

"Well, that's all well and good," Laura-Mae said, her voice prim. "But we won't be sharing information with you, Kris, I'm terribly sorry."

"No big loss." Kris's voice was light but Sebastian detected a slight quaver to it.

He caught Kris's eye and gave them an encouraging smile, which they returned with a subtle eyeroll.

Sebastian tucked into breakfast, ignoring the tightness in his gut. He had to eat for strength, and he needed strength to get through this weekend.

"If you don't mind my asking, what does a familiar do, for a mage?" Basil asked. "I was thinking of getting a familiar at one time, myself."

"Oh, they're wonderful. They enhance magic, they help with awakening and growing magical gifts, and they're super intelligent, to boot." Kris pulled a wallet out of their polka dot overalls and pulled out a polaroid picture of a huge shaggy black and brown dog.

"Sweet," Basil said, then handed it to Sebastian.

"That's not a dog, that's a bear," Sebastian joked. He handed the picture to Horatio who made a soft 'awwww' sound.

"I get that a lot." Kris took the picture back and filed it away. "He's very cute but he doesn't really know how large he is."

Laura-Mae cleared her throat, everyone looked at her. "How sure are you that this so-called familiar isn't a demonic entity?"

Kris rolled their eyes. "I am not having this conversation. I know what he is and it has nothing to do with demons. Not everything you see is demons, okay?"

Laura-Mae's expression turned sour. "Well, I never."

"Please," Horatio said, making a quelling gesture with both hands. "No magical politics at the breakfast table? I'm not awake enough for this."

"Agreed," Kris said.

"A very good policy," Basil said. "I'm sorry for asking about it."

"It's fine," Horatio said. "But we have a lot of differences in opinions here, and I don't want fights on the second day."

"Of course, we don't mean nothing," Randall said, all good old boy smarm and manners. "Consider the subject dropped."

"Thank you." Horatio went back to their croissant.

Everyone ate in silence for a few minutes, Sebastian deliberately watching the Rhodes couple in case they tried to bring something up again. Basil focused entirely on his food, as did Kris.

"Is it all right if we interview your service staff, Horatio?" Sebastian asked, once he'd polished off his muesli.

"Fine with me, although it's up to them if they consent or not," Horatio said.

"Of course, I wouldn't have it any other way," Sebastian nodded. "Thank you."

Basil

"I don't have much to say," Mindy said, when Sebastian asked her about the interview. "I don't mind you filming me, but I'm really only here a few hours to vacuum the floors and take the laundry out. The windows are done monthly by a specialist."

Sebastian gestured for her to sit in the seat he'd arranged near the window for the best light. Mindy sat primly, crossing her ankles.

"Can you please introduce yourself?"

"Mindy, I'm the cleaner here, part time."

Basil noticed she didn't give a last name, and Sebastian didn't prompt her. Respecting her privacy perhaps?

"Is there a reason you don't stay more than a couple of hours? Andrew and Eve live here and I'm sure they get paid well for it." Mindy twisted her fingers together. "Horatio is a very kind and generous boss, but I wouldn't sleep in this house for anything in the world."

"Can you tell me why?"

Basil adjusted the camera, feeling for the woman. The house had a horrible aura, anyone could tell that.

Mindy swallowed. "Everyone in the area knows Beach House is cursed. There are stories of strange lights and sounds after dark, and the doors slam themselves shut. I've seen it, even in daylight. I'm not a superstitious woman, but I know when I'm not welcome and I'll tell you honestly, no one living is welcome in Beach House."

Basil shivered lightly, he entirely agreed with Mindy.

"Can you talk a little more about what you've seen?"

Mindy uncrossed her ankles. "Doors slamming shut on their own, mostly, but I'm sure I've seen some of the paintings change as well. I've never been able to prove it, though, and Horatio took down the old Crane family portraits. It was the best thing to do, in the circumstances."

"Do you know where they got stored?"

Mindy shook her head. "Look I've really got to get to work."

"Thank you for your time." Sebastian shook her hand and gave her a warm smile. He looked directly into the camera after she left and widened his eyes, puffing his cheeks out in a 'that was a lot' gesture.

Next up was Andrew, who had a very skeptical expression as he walked in. He also introduced himself with only a first name, and then folded his arms.

"This place? It's a job. All old houses have weird noises, it's called settling. We get a heavy rain and none of the doors open for a day and a half, leaks somewhere although I've never been able to find them. This ghost stuff is a load of bull crap."

Sebastian nodded. "There's a lot of people I've spoken to who feel the same."

"Yeah, so, how about you don't waste too much more of our time? I don't want to get behind."

"One last thing," Sebastian said. "Horatio said they'd heard a lot of knocking in the night, up and down the hallways. Have you ever heard that?"

Andrew looked down and shook his head. "Never."

"And you wouldn't know anything that could cause something like that?"

Now Andrew looked directly at Sebastian. "I'm not the kind to go around at night making weird noises to spook my employer, if that's what you're getting at."

Sebastian raised his hands. "Not at all. Thanks for giving us your time."

Eve refused an interview, saying she had too much to do, cooking for all the guests, and neither Basil nor Sebastian wanted to pressure her.

Sebastian

"Ugh, after all that I need a rest," Basil said. "I might sniff out that library Horatio mentioned and have some quiet time, if you don't mind."

Sebastian kissed his boyfriend on the cheek. "Of course I don't mind, I can hardly keep you away from books."

Basil blushed slightly and smiled. "Thanks. Come find me if you need, okay?"

Sebastian watched his boyfriend hurry off and rubbed his arm. What would he do? He could walk around the gardens perhaps, film some atmospheric stuff and images of the house for cutaways? Or he could go and take a nap. It was still early in the day but the presence of the house was draining him in a way he didn't want to admit.

Outside might be the best idea then. He went back to The Blue Room to put away most of his filming gear, going with only a handheld camcorder for his walk outside. He pulled on a heavy flannel shirt — the autumn wind could have a chill to it — and made his way down and out the front door.

The front door was open, standing slightly ajar, possibly to air out the house, possibly to save guests the trouble of locking and unlocking it.

Whatever the reason, Sebastian breathed easier once he'd stepped over the threshold.

The sun was out, and although it wasn't exactly hot, it warmed his head and shoulders pleasantly. There was barely any breeze, just enough to make him glad he'd layered on the flannel.

Instead of filming right away, Sebastian walked down a path that led away from the driveway where the cars were parked. Situated on the coastal cliff, the gardens weren't the traditional English style roses and lush lawns that he sometimes associated with large old houses, but scrubby grass, and stands of native trees and bushes. Sebastian recognised several ti kōuka, or cabbage trees, along with puka closer to the house. As he took the path down the side of the house towards the cliffs, toitoi proliferated, its tall, feathered spikes distinctive. It felt good to have such familiar plants and trees there, he imagined the local wildlife loved it too. The nearest neighbours, as far as he could tell from driving in yesterday, were some distance off. Definitely outside of shouting distance, although he could probably walk to the next place.

Isolated. He wondered how Horatio had coped, presumably they'd lived here alone before taking on staff. It must have been very lonely.

The side of the house that overlooked the cliffs had a large verandah with some outdoor furniture, Andrew sat in one of the chairs smoking. He waved at Sebastian.

"Need anything?"

Sebastian shook his head. "Nah, man. You keep on relaxing. I'm wandering without direction."

Andrew nodded and sat back in the wicker chair, letting his gaze slip back to the horizon.

Sebastian hurried his pace, not wanting to intrude any more on Andrew's time. The path split, one headed towards the cliff edge, about thirty metres away, and the other around the house. Sebastian took the fork around the house, not quite ready to stand at the cliff's edge.

He wasn't his usual self, he knew that. The house was certainly an influence on his mood, but the events of the previous months, all boiling down to being transformed into a cat, it had added a dullness to his spark.

It made it slightly harder to get up in the mornings. His mind had begun to spiral more often, imagining terrible things happening. Primarily magic going wrong, or running into Asher again.

Standing on a cliff-edge didn't feel dangerous, exactly, he had no intention of hurting himself in any way, but he didn't want to hear the dark thoughts that might crop up if he did stand there.

Instead, he did the thing that grounded him. He flicked on the camera, set it on his shoulder, and took a spanning panorama of the view of the back yard and the cliff, with the ocean beyond.

With the camera on his shoulder, he made his way further around the path, saying nothing, letting the birdsong and the crunch of footsteps on gravel be the only narration.

The gardens on this side of the manor had a more manicured look to them, the paths paved with large cobbles, the lawn a different variety of grass, more manicured looking. Ahead there were some smaller buildings, ones that had been obscured from view by the trees and bushes beside the driveway.

"Perhaps an old stables..." Sebastian mused. "Or servant's quarters? Maybe garden sheds?"

A figure crossed from the shadow of the Manor, towards the small buildings, startling Sebastian. He had for a moment, lost in thoughts, imagined himself entirely alone out in that desolate place.

He recognised Horatio, and his heart slowed down.

Horatio didn't seem to have seen him. Their shoulders were hunched in a thick black cardigan, and their head was down.

Sebastian dropped the camera to his side and turned it off. "Horatio?"

The figure startled, turned towards him and then raised a hand to wave. "Sebastian?"

"Yes," he sped up, closing the distance between them.

Horatio waited, patiently enough. "What are you up to out here?"

"Filming atmosphere," Sebastian said. "For cutaways, but sometimes I pick something up when I watch the footage back." He felt like he was speaking rehearsed lines, hiding what he'd been pondering just before. He didn't like admitting to the darkness he felt inside him.

Horatio nodded. "Very good. I was headed to the old chapel, want to see it?"

A chapel? Even better. "Definitely. That sounds haunted for sure."

Horatio chuckled drily and turned to lead the way to one of the smaller buildings, it was mostly hidden from view, until they took the path that led directly to it. Then Sebastian saw the small wooden cross nailed to the front. "What are the other buildings?"

Horatio nodded at the closer one. "Vicarage, and then garden shed, although both of them get used as sheds now. The last tenants let the chapel get full of rubbish, but the first thing I did was clear it out."

"Are you religious?" Sebastian asked gently. Religion was a tricky subject, he'd been raised with Christian and Māori faiths, and Basil of course, was dedicated to his parents' brand of Wicca.

"I was, once." Horatio said, their voice dreamlike. "I grew up with it, but I gave it up as a teenager. I believe in spirits, in the universe, but I don't believe there's one big guy up in the sky watching over us."

"But you cleared out the chapel?"

Horatio paused with their hand on the ancient-looking brass door handle. "Yes. I like it to be clean and clear, it's a sacred space, even if just because people thought of it that way in the past. Besides, it has a nice aura to it."

They gave Sebastian a rueful smile and opened the door, leading him inside.

Sebastian felt what they meant immediately. Unlike the house proper, this space felt light and airy. He felt his shoulders relax, and his chest loosen. He took a deep breath and let it out with a whoosh. "It's lovely."

"It's my little getaway."

Sebastian watched them, his fingers itching to start recording but mindful of Horatio's preferences and resisting the urge. He slipped the camera into its case and set it down on the bench near the door.

"How did you come to own this place, anyway? If you don't mind me asking..."

Horatio gave him a soft smile and sat down at the pew closest to where the old altar must have stood. There was no altar now, but a modest stained glass window set into the back wall let in some filtered sunlight. It did feel peaceful in there. Sacred. Sebastian could sense the mana of the place, of the people who had built and blessed it.

"I don't mind. I have nothing to do with the family who used to own it. I came into some money, some inheritance from a great aunt back in England, and I sold an app I'd built, and this place came up on the market at the right time."

"You're from England then?" Sebastian couldn't detect any hint of accent to Horatio's words, but that didn't necessarily mean anything.

"No, my family is, but my parents were born in New Zealand, my grandparents moved over from London right after they got married. They settled in Hamilton, then sort of gradually moved North."

"Do you see them much, or... sorry are they still around?"

"They're still alive, but I don't see them much. Them or my sister and her family. None of them really understand about my gender, you know? They think... I don't know, I guess they thought it was a phase, and then when I didn't just magically grow out of it they don't know how to deal with me."

"I'm sorry," Sebastian said. His own parents weren't exactly poster children for great parenting but at least they accepted him — insomuch as they thought of him at all. He let the silence stretch out, and Horatio countered with their own question.

"How about your parents? I bet they love Basil."

"They've never met him," Sebastian said. "They're alive, but they're business consultants, high flyers, big names... they're always travelling. They send me money, I'm basically on an allowance from them, which is why I can run around ghost-hunting instead of like, keeping a real job. But I almost never speak to them. I sometimes wonder why they had me at all, you know? They put me in boarding school when I was fourteen and they sold the house I grew up in."

Horatio hummed to themself.

Sebastian sighed, talking about his parents brought up an ache. He usually felt like the poor little rich boy, whining about his parents giving him money instead of attention, but Horatio seemed to understand.

"Sucks." Horation finally offered up.

"It really does." Sebastian had to bring up the bright side though. "At least I have Basil's parents, now. They live on Waiheke."

Horatio smiled, a touch of sadness to it. "That sounds nice."

"You're really going to live here all alone? Sounds, well, lonely."

Horatio chuckled. "Well, I'm going to get back on the dating scene, see if I can't find a partner or two to move in."

Sebastian smiled and bumped his shoulder gently against theirs. "That's the spirit. Any likely parties invited to this ghost hunt?"

Horatio chuckled. "Well, Kris is cute, don't you think? I don't know what they're into though and given the circumstances coming onto them is a bit uncool."

"You can still spend time with them, though."

"I could." Horatio nodded. "What do you think's going on, anyway?"

"Oh I think this place is definitely haunted," Sebastian said. "I don't have any recorded proof yet, but it's already messing with Basil. He's kind of a magnet for weird shit, to be honest."

Horatio's mouth tugged up on one side. "Good to know it's not all in my imagination."

"We'll get to the bottom of it."

Horatio nodded again. "What do you think that means in terms of the afterlife?"

Sebastian whistled softly. "Big question. From what I've experienced there's two types of spirits — those that need something resolved so they can move on, and those who actively want to remain on Earth. Basil and I have helped a fair few on their way to letting go, but where they go after that? I have no idea."

Horatio hummed. "I tried asking Laura-Mae that and she said it's all angels and demons. I like your answer better."

It took all of the diplomacy Sebastian possessed to reply, "Everyone seems to believe different things, don't they?"

Horatio narrowed their eyes, a smirk playing at the corners of their mouth. Sebastian wanted to wrap his arms around them and invite them to Christmas with Basil's parents, they'd all get on so well, but they still barely knew each other.

"What do you hope happens? Or, where do you think they go?"

Sebastian didn't answer right away. He didn't really know... his childhood had been a mix of being told about Heaven and Hell, and the tree way up north where dead spirits passed into the underworld under the ocean. "I don't know," he said. "I hope, it's either oblivion, or something beautiful. In some ways a definitive ending sounds pleasant, but if there is an underworld, or a spirit realm, I hope it's a beautiful, fulfilling place. Somewhere with trees and oceans and there's time enough to do whatever you like, or nothing at all."

Horatio hummed in agreement. "That sounds good to me. I'm in, either way it goes. Do you want to start a cult, or do you perhaps have a newsletter I could subscribe to?"

Sebastian laughed, the sound suddenly louder than how they'd been speaking. "No, but I do have this badass YouTube channel."

Horatio grinned. "Okay, I've watched some of them, it's how I found you, but I hereby pledge to like, comment, and subscribe. Maybe I'll even donate to your page."

"I appreciate it."

Sebastian realised he'd invited himself along to what was surely their quiet contemplation time. "Anyway, I'll leave you to it. It's been really nice, no, lovely talking with you." "You too, Sebastian," Horatio turned to face him as he stood. "Please, use this place any time you need it, okay?"

"Thank you." Sebastian grabbed his camera on the way out and made his way back to the Manor.

CHAPTER EIGHT

BASIL

B asil found the library. There was, to his professional eye, a clear demarcation between the books inherited from the previous owners, and Horatio's own additions. The rows of leather bound volumes with matching gold embossed titles lined the shelves in the back of the library, and Horatio's more modern books took up a half-full shelf closer to the door, and made up some stacks on the low coffee tables.

The room smelled like old books, dust and old paper, absolutely divine and familiar to Basil's nose. There was a fireplace in the back wall with a generous brick hearth, ensuring space between the flames and the precious stock of the room. The room had hardwood flooring but it was largely covered by Turkish rugs in rich jewel reds and greens, and there were armchairs positioned in four spots so you could stop and read at any place in the room.

He took a deep breath and relaxed. He knew where he stood with books, far more comfortable than with strangers, or people talking about demons.

The fire was burning low and the room was pleasantly warm as a result. Basil made his way to the shelves of older books. Sometimes places like this had books of family history, or journals or similar from the past that could shed light into the spiritual activity.

He perused the shelves, pleased to find the fiction was organised alphabetically by author with Austen at the start, leading through the Brontes, Dante, and down to Tolstoy and the like. These were the staples of any fancy person's library, and wouldn't help with the investigation though. Much as his fingers itched for him to pick up and sample some of the poetry of Wordsworth.

He crossed the room to the other side and picked up a large book with the word *Bible* on the spine. It looked old enough that perhaps it was a family bible, which would mean... Yes, he opened the cover to find evidence of a hand-inked family tree. Only...

It was only evidence of it, ink soaked through onto pages, and the ragged evidence of the end pages of the book torn out. Someone had forcibly removed the family tree from this bible.

Frowning, Basil flipped through the pages, then ruffled the book to see if anything would fall out. He had a vague hope someone had found the torn pages and stuffed them back into the book — but no such luck.

The dots of ink that had soaked through taught him very little. He could barely make out the family name, in fact the only words he was sure of were 'family tree'. He sighed, and slid the bible back into its slot on the shelf.

"Hope you don't mind my intrusion."

The voice startled him and he turned, his heart in his mouth.

Kris stood there, shoulders hunched and cheeks pink. "Sorry, I just... things felt like I should be in here."

Basil startled, flapping his hands, trying to recover himself. "Yes, of course, please do come in, of course."

"Thanks," Kris closed the door behind them and walked closer. "Find anything, yet?"

"No especially, I found the bible but someone's torn out the family tree. I was hoping it might shed some light on things."

"Do you mind if I take a look at it?"

"Of course not," Basil pulled the bible down again and held it out for Kris to take. They held it in both their hands and sat in the nearest armchair. "I could try and look through its past, see if I can read the page that used to be there, that'd be useful right?"

"Very," Basil bit his lip, this kind of thing would be the kind of thing Sebastian would want to film — usually — but as it involved mage magic, it might also make him too nervous. He decided against letting Sebastian know, figuring he could report on it all to camera if needed.

He watched closely as Kris set the book in their lap, shoved their sleeves up and withdrew a beaded bracelet off their left wrist. They held the beads in one hand and placed the other flat on the cover of the book. Their lips moved, muttering some words of invocation.

A moment later Basil's own magic responded to the thrum of power that came from Kris. Their hair fluttered as if in a sudden wind. They bent their head, eyes closed, and for a few long seconds they remained in that attitude.

With a gasp, they flicked their head up and looked directly at Basil. "Crane family tree!"

Basil blinked. "Crane family? Good, that's good."

"I saw I think one other name, Hugh. I couldn't see much over his shoulder."

Basil pulled out the notebook and pen he carried in his waistcoat pocket and scribbled down *Hugh Crane*. "That's really good, thank you." He slowly processed what they'd said. "You were looking over his shoulder?" "Yes," Kris said. They moved the bible to the table and scrubbed at their face with one hand. "Seeing through time can be very direct like that sometimes, I looked into the time when the family tree was being written and I saw a man with a pen and inkwell writing. I couldn't see well over his shoulder, he was so hunched up."

Basil couldn't help a smile. "You saw him? Like you actually travelled in time?"

"Yes, in a sense." Kris returned the smile. "That's not how you do things?"

"No," Basil sat in the closest chair. "I've been able to summon echoes of the past but it's not like that, not really. I'm not physically there."

"I suppose I wasn't either." Kris slipped the bracelet back on. "My body remains here, but I suppose it's a part of me that moves, that can observe. Time magic can be dangerous though, you don't want to affect things or alter anything."

"Of course not."

"Although." Kris frowned, looking around. "He was in this room but the layout was different, there was a desk where he was sitting, obviously, but the shelves..." Kris stood up and went to the wall of shelves on the left hand side. "These were angled differently."

Basil followed her, the shadow of a discovery blooming in his mind. "Angled differently how? They're built into the wall."

"I think maybe..." Kris ran their hand along a selection of matching poetry collections and their fingers rested on one in particular.

Basil's breath caught as Kris yanked on the spine of the book. There was a click and the shelf swung towards them.

"Hidden door!" Basil breathed, absolutely delighted. "I've always, always wanted to do that," Kris said. "It was everything I'd hoped for."

"Well, what's behind it?" Basil couldn't contain his excitement. It was like being in a movie, and he wanted to know the next clue.

Kris swung the door further open and they both stepped behind into a small room, this one lined with books that made Basil's arms come out in gooseflesh. These weren't just books of classic fiction, these were books of magic.

Basil pulled out his cellphone and flicked on the flashlight app to light up some of the room. Kris conjured a small, glowing orb into their hand. "A secret stash of mystical books," Kris murmured. "This is so badass."

Basil resisted the urge to run his fingers over these books, instead reading the titles on the spines. *Witchcraft For Use In The House, The Tarot Arts, Small Hexes, Demons by Name, A Chronicle of the Fae Folk, Unbreakable Curses, the Magicks of Dissolving...* Some of these weren't titles that Basil would stock in his library. The reason his body was reacting the way it had was because of the nature of the contents of the books. On some level his own magic could sense the ill intentions of these works. They weren't all bad, not by a long shot, but the bad ones were... a lot.

"Hugh was a witch?"

"Or a mage," Kris said. "And a curious one, who didn't mind dabbling in the more evil stuff."

Basil whistled. "This could account for some of the ill-feeling in the house. Simply storing this many books together with no discernible wards or protections..." he went back to the doorframe created by the open bookshelf to check, but there were no runes, sigils, even a dried leaf of herb. It was simply a door frame, and the magic books shut within. He walked back in to Kris. "Nothing."

"It's dangerous..." Kris said. "Some of these books, if they fell into the wrong hands..."

Before he could answer, the bookshelf slammed shut and Basil's cell phone went dead in his hands. Kris's light orb flared brighter for a second and then went out as well.

"No, no," Kris said, their voice urgent. "I don't like being shut in small spaces."

"There must be a handle on the inside." Basil turned to run his hands over the door, and found it completely smooth. "Oh no."

"Don't say 'oh no'," they pushed past Basil and from the scrabbling noises were trying to find a way out.

Basil tried to summon the well of magic that had been prickling him moments before but he could sense nothing. It was exactly like when Asher had cut off his magic from him. He bit his lip, pressed the power button on his cell phone and prayed it would turn on. After a moment's delay, it did. "I'll call Sebastian for help," he said.

"This can't happen, I can't—" Kris gasped. "I can't breathe."

"It's all right, there's plenty of air in here." Basil tried to make his voice as soothing as possible. "Just relax, can you access any of your magic?"

Kris stopped moving. "Magic. Right."

The phone start screen loaded and Basil tapped to Sebastian's number and hit dial.

"Open," Kris said. Nothing happened. They said it again, and again.

"Whatever it is I think it's cut us off—"

"Hello?" Sebastian said over the phone speakers. "Bastian, we're in the library, in a hidden room and we can't get out," Basil said as quickly but as clearly as he could. "Can you come find us?" "On my way. How do I find the room?"

"The bookcase with the green leather bound poetry books."

Kris was repeated 'open' again and again. Basil touched them lightly on the shoulder. "Kris which book did you pull on?"

"I don't know," Kris sounded irritated. "Something... open!"

"Please, Kris, Sebastian can get us out, he just needs to know which book."

Kris stilled again, breathing heavily. "I think it was … I can't remember, hold on…" Kris took an audible breath. "Something about goblins?" Basil didn't have to think too long. "The Goblin Market? Christina Rosetti?" "Yes!" Kris slumped to the ground, dimly lit by the glow of Basil's phone.

"Goblin Market, okay, I'll be right there."

"Stay on the line," Basil said. "Kris isn't good in small spaces."

Sebastian started to reply when Basil's phone shut down again and would not turn back on. Basil crouched beside Kris and tried to coach them to breathe, slowly and steadily. "It'll be okay, just in and out, Sebastian's on his way." "It's cold though, so cold," Kris's breath was easing but Basil could hear the shake in their voice. Now that they'd said it, he did feel the chill.

"Come on, we'll hug to stay warm," he said.

Kris was instantly under his arm, pressing against him. He could feel the shudders wracking their body. *Sebastian, please get here soon! Whoever or whatever has done this doesn't seem to like us much and without my magic I don't know what else to do.*

It could have been merely seconds or it could have been an hour. He knew Sebastian wouldn't have taken that long to get to them, but there was every possibility the magical atmosphere with all those books had dilated time. He held onto Kris and tried to say soothing things, but soon they were both so cold it was all they could do to hold one another and shiver.

The door swung open after a time that Basil couldn't possibly have measured.

The light from the library, not to mention the heat from the fire was as welcome as the sight of Sebastian's concerned face. He immediately crouched and took Kris's elbow, helping them up and to the chair closest to the fire.

Basil went to follow and felt his knees buckle. He edged on his bottom to the doorway, determined not to let it close again even if it meant wedging it with his own body.

Sebastian returned a moment later and scooped Basil up in his arms. Basil blushed, even in the circumstances. Sebastian didn't show off his strength like this often and it always took Basil's breath away.

Sebastian positioned him in the armchair facing Kris and added some logs to the fire.

"Thank you, love," Basil said, pulling his knees up to his chest. "That was... intense."

Kris had completely relaxed. "Thank you, and sorry for freaking out. Little spaces aren't that bad, but being shut in one?" They shuddered. "Worst nightmare."

"No need to apologise," Basil said. "It was frightening."

***

Sebastian

He brought them tea and little cakes from the snack sideboard and soon both Basil and Kris had rallied enough to explain what had happened.

"A hidden room of magic books, that has to be important," he agreed. He picked up his camera and changed out the memory card for a fresh one, stowing the one with the cliff footage in the camera bag. "Basil, do you think you could demonstrate the way it opened? Or would you rather film me doing it?"

Basil sipped the last of his tea and set the cup down. "Much as I'm loathe to go in there again, I think I have to be the one doing the reveal of the bookshelf," Basil said. "It's too good."

"I'll stay right here," Kris said vehemently. "Although, when you've filmed what you want, we ought to put some wards and protections on that thing."

"Agreed," Basil said. "Do you mind me filming you doing that? It'd be nice to show what method you use," Sebastian asked.

Kris helped themselves to another cake. "That's fine."

Basil talked through the discovery in front of the bookshelf and pulled on *Goblin Market and Other Verses* to demonstrate the way the shelf swing out.

Even with the ordeal he'd been through, Basil's face lit up at the reveal of the room and Sebastian knew it would be something he'd talk about for years to come. Every librarian's dream, a hidden bookcase door.

Sebastian smiled, following to block the open door as Basil stepped into the small room. It was dim in there, and there was no sign of a light switch so Sebastian did the best he could with the ambient light from the library. He made a note to come back with one of his standing lights and get better footage of the books, but that would wait.

Basil, an absolute natural at speaking to camera by this point, explained the titles of the books they'd found and his concerns over the natures of them. He explained the dampening effect the room or the books had on his magic and Kris's as well, despite them having different sorts of magic, or at least, different approaches.

Sebastian gave him a thumbs up and flicked the camera off as Basil wound down. "Do you and Kris have inherently different magics or is it more about how you use it?" Sebastian asked, too curious to be nervous about magic.

"I'm not really sure," Basil said.

Kris hopped up at the sound of their name and joined them. "It's an age-old question, that," they said. "I'm certain, from what I've learned and other mages I've spoken to, that all magic comes from the same source, but in practice witches and mages have such different ways of handling it... it could be an innate thing, or it could be more in how you're trained. If you're found first by a mage or a witch..."

Basil hummed. "There is crossover in the things we do, I've seen mages using herbs and salt and so on, but as a witch I don't need a focus like you do."

Kris rubbed the stack of beaded bracelets on their wrist. "But witches sometimes use wands and familiars, that's the same thing really."

The frown on Basil's face showed he hadn't considered that.

Sebastian bit his lip so he didn't smile too wide and put them off. "Perhaps we could get some insight from you two working together on this?"

Kris smiled and offered their hand to Basil — showing no hard feelings. Basil didn't hesitate, he took their hand and pulled them into a hug. "I think it's very important," he said, half into their shoulder and half to camera, "that witches and mages have better communication and relations. Splitting apart because of our approaches is foolish."

"Well said, Basil."

Sebastian filmed as the two of them wove magic together. Basil had a pen, which they used to etch runes into the doorframe and between them they spoke a variety of words and incantations. Sebastian saw the runes glow briefly, and in his chest he felt a strange new sensation. Almost like a pulling from deep inside his ribcage. It vanished the same moment the runes stopped glowing, and he licked his lips, not liking it but not sure what to do about it.

A creak came from the wall and then the ceiling, Beach House settling, or shifting a little perhaps.

Sebastian shivered involuntarily and the other two glanced around. The noises stopped and the bookshelf swung slowly shut again.

"Well, that appears to be that," Basil said, dusting off his hands. "Kris, would you be willing to do an interview to camera now, or would you rather another time?" Sebastian asked.

"Ah, now is fine, we're all here and you have the camera out, after all."

Sebastian arranged them by the fireside, the flickering flames casting a flattering light over them. He positioned himself close to the fire so the light was correct. Basil took over the filming and Sebastian sat beside Kris.

"This is Kris Crimson, a local mage," he said. Kris waved hesitantly at the camera. "How about we start with, what were you doing when you got the invitation to Beach House?"

"Ah nothing very exciting," Kris said. "I was making myself lunch, I think. The mail is delivered directly through my front door via a mail slot, so I heard it right away and read it as I ate my sandwich."

Sebastian nodded, pleased that their answer was so mundane and straightforward when compared to Laura-Mae's.

"What made you decide to come?"

"It sounded interesting," Kris shrugged. "I didn't have anything else pressing to do and who can resist being invited to a big old house in the middle of nowhere to see some ghosts?"

"Have you seen ghosts before?"

Kris shook their head. "No, my speciality — mages tend to focus on one special aspect of magic, I don't know if witches do the same?"

"Sort of," Basil said, from behind the camera. "We usually have a talent we lean into."

"Right, well my specialities are twofold, fibres and fire." "Can you explain a bit more about what that means?" Sebastian leaned closer, relaxing into the interview.

"Fibres, like, the power of knotting or weaving threads together, what it means to an object to be mended with a patch, and the magic power that thread and fabric can contain. For example, this pair of patchwork pants has spells sewn into it, I can use those stitches as a focus for my magic. Fire is more easily explained, using a flame to focus, and then enhance or reduce the power of fire itself."

Sebastian found himself looking over the patches and small pieces of embroidery on Kris's pants. He had assumed it was just a quirky fashion statement, but to know that it served a magical purpose? Well, he was impressed.

"That's amazing." "Thank you. If you like I could sew a patch or two into a piece of your clothing? For protection, or extra strength or the like. It only works while the garment is being worn, of course."

"Maybe." Sebastian tried to imagine how it'd feel to wear a piece of magic, but... he trusted Kris. He knew they wouldn't do anything to hurt him. "I'll see what I brought with me."

Basil made a noise and Sebastian looked up to meet his eyes. He was pleased, his eyes almost shiny. Sebastian blushed a little, and turned back to Kris.

"I don't know how much I'll be able to help with the hauntings at Beach House," Kris said. "But I can verify that they're happening, that something incredibly weird is going on here."

Sebastian guided Kris to explain what they'd seen and heard.

The interview ended with them shaking hands. It had already been an eventful day and sunset was still a ways off.

Sebastian packed up his filming equipment. "Could I get your phone number?" Basil asked. "I'd like to stay in touch."

"No phone, sorry," Kris said. "It's really hard to stop my magic frying them. I guess that's a difference between mages and witches we didn't consider."

CHAPTER NINE

SEBASTIAN

They went to the Blue Room to stow the camera gear. Sebastian put his camera batteries on to charge. Basil had borrowed a few books from the library that he set on the bedside table, along with the books he'd brought from home.

"Still an hour before cocktails," Basil said.

"Let's go for a walk in the garden," Sebastian said. "It's pretty out there, and I bet you could use the fresh air."

"A fine idea."

Sebastian offered Basil his arm, and they made their way outside. Sebastian felt more grounded. More himself. Maybe the conversation with Horatio had done it, or maybe it was getting to rescue Basil and then do a relatively normal interview.

Whatever the reason, stepping out with Basil into the bright autumn sunshine felt like everything was right in the world. For the moment, at least.

He led Basil to the back of the manor to see the outlook over the cliffs.

"Tonight we should pay careful attention," Basil said. "I think we'll see more activity, especially after the library."

"I think you're right. I wonder what the scientist is doing, we should check in on her, don't you think?"

Basil hummed, his gaze on the ocean. "Probably taking temperature readings and so on? It's beautiful out here, isn't it?"

"Reminds me of looking out to the ocean with you in Napier." Sebastian took Basil's hand and squeezed it. "I know I've not been... my usual self, lately. I'm sorry about it. I want to work through it all, get back to normal."

Basil leaned his head on Sebastian's shoulder. "What's normal, for us? I mean, you literally hunt ghosts for a living and I'm a witch, born and bred. You're allowed to freak out, to learn, to heal, or not. I don't mind, I'm here for you whatever you need."

Sebastian's chest tightened with love, pride that his boyfriend was so wonderfully trusting and perfect. "Thank you."

"Did you see that?"

They turned at the sound of the unfamiliar voice to see Wendla coming around the corner. She was dressed in a vintage skirt suit, something fancy like Chanel, perhaps? Sebastian thought he recognised the cut of it.

She held vape in one hand, and took a deep hit from it.

"See what?"

Wendla exhaled a plume of white smoke and hooked her thumb over her shoulder. "Back on the lawn, apparitions."

"No?" Basil pulled away from Sebastian. "Where? Can you show us."

"Of course, do you want to film it, Mr Black?"

"I left my camera stuff," Sebastian said. "And just call me Sebastian."

"Ah well, I'll show you anyway." Wendla took the lead, walking down the path to the side of the house the chapel was on.

There was a nicely trimmed lawn past the small buildings, with some low bushes and flowerbeds surrounding it.

"They were there," Wendla said. "Just watch."

Sebastian held his breath. "They?"

"Mmm."

Something flickered in the air, like a static picture cutting in and out. Sebastian thought he saw the shape of a person, no, three people. It cut out again as soon as he'd registered the shapes.

"Did you see that?" Basil turned to Sebastian, eyes bright. "You can't always see spirits."

"I saw something," Sebastian added. "Three people?"

"Yes, three children, I thought as well," Wendla said. "Perhaps having a picnic? There was the hint of a blanket." She strode onto the grass, pointing at the area where Sebastian had seen a shadow.

"I didn't see that much detail." Sebastian pulled out his phone to film — it was better than nothing. Wendla folded her arms and looked around as the figures appeared once more. She was standing in amongst them.

"Can you feel them?" Basil asked.

Wendla nodded, apparently not at all phased by her proximity to the ghosts. She looked down at them critically. "Got something to say? Do you? Hello?"

The ghosts flickered out again.

"I thought I heard laughter," Basil said.

Wendla shrugged. "I think visions, not proper apparitions, perhaps? They didn't respond to my questions."

Sebastian saw her shiver as she took another drag from her vape. "Maybe you should come away from there, Wendla." "Ah, they can't hurt me." She walked back towards them all the same. "But if it makes you more comfortable."

"I guess it does, yeah, thank you."

"Not at all." Wendla stood beside Sebastian and folded her arms. "Strange to see them in daylight, I wonder what it means."

Basil looked around, up and down the path. "No one else around, eh?"

"No. Just us lucky three." Wendla smacked her lips. "Pity. If those so-called demonologists were here we could expose them for the frauds they are."

Sebastian chuckled. "Laura-Mae and Randall didn't make a good impression on you?"

"I should say not. They're in the corridor upstairs at the moment, and she's scribbling on pieces of paper when anyone with half a third eye can see there's nothing happening in *there*." She snorted, a some-how quite elegant sound from her, and tossed her hair.

"Kris caught me up on your adventure in the library, so Francois is there now seeing if he can't communicate. We'll let you know if we discover anything."

Wendla was the real deal, not just in terms of actual psychic ability and knowledge, but she wasn't viewing the weekend as a competition between experts.

"I feel sorry for the scientist though," Wendla went on. "Poor thing already has a handful of things she can't explain. Maybe I'll go get her, she if she can rationalise this…"

The picnickers appeared again, more solidly this time, and they remained. Sebastian caught his breath, filming the patch of grass, uncertain if his phone would capture it.

It was three children, dressed in Victorian garb. The boy looked the eldest at maybe ten or eleven, in black short pants and a tidy shirt, his hair slicked to one side. The two girls were sitting demurely in frilled white dresses with large ribbons in their hair. The smallest girl, perhaps six or seven years old, was weaving daisy chains together.

Sebastian's heart raced, hardly able to believe the detail of the vision, the indisputable truth that the ghosts had shown themselves to him, when often it was only sound and object movement that Sebastian could detect.

Then, as one, the children turned their heads to face the onlookers. Each face was stony, their eyes black, and voidlike.

A chill shot up Sebastian's spine and he couldn't help shuddering. Gripping his phone with his hand to ensure he didn't drop it, he suppressed a gasp.

Basil took his elbow, a warm hand, steadying as they both stepped back.

"That is interesting," Wendla didn't sound bothered by the change in the apparitions. "I think they've officially noticed us now."

The ghosts vanished from view, but something told Sebastian they hadn't actually gone anywhere.

"We should get out of here," Sebastian's voice sounded strangled.

"Come on, inside," Basil said. He turned Sebastian away with a firm grip on his arm.

"I'll come along too, I'm not entirely sure what to make of that." Wendla was a pleasant companion, keeping up small talk and distracting Sebastian from his fears enough that he could breathe easily by the time they got to the main foyer.

"You must come along to cocktail hour, Francois and I want to get to know you better," Wendla said. She took Sebastian's hand between her gloved ones and pressed them warmly. "It'll be fun."

"Yes, of course. A stiff drink is just what I need."

"Perhaps you could interview Wendla and Francois, both before dinner?" Basil prompted.

"Sounds divine," Wendla said. "I must go change, see you soon."

She swept up the stairs, and Basil shook his head. "She's like someone out of fifties Hollywood or something."

"She's divine." Sebastian chuckled. Her favourite superlative suited her best. "I bet she's changing for dinner."

Basil pressed his hand to his chest. "Should we change, too?"

"I didn't bring enough clothes to sustain dressing for dinner, love."

Basil chuckled, although his expression was slightly disappointed. "I guess I didn't either."

"But we do have a little time. You could read for a half hour before we come back. I know you have quite the to-read pile."

"Perfect, you know me so well." Basil kissed Sebastian's cheek and they went back to their room.

*** Basil

The parlour was warm from the roaring fire. Horatio was nowhere to be seen, but Wendla and Francois were presiding over the room and a fully stocked drinks cart with wide smiles. Brit, the scientist, was seated near the window, nursing something orange, and Kris waved from an armchair by the fire.

"Basil and Sebastian, welcome, welcome!" Francois boomed. "Thank you for joining us."

"Wouldn't miss it for the world," Sebastian said. He'd taken the time to shave before coming down and he looked particularly handsome to Basil.

Wendla had indeed changed into a cocktail dress, a deep forest green, off-the-shoulder number that clung to all her curves. Francois had a black velvet jacket over his matching green waistcoat and suit pants.

Basil felt underdressed. He adjusted his shirt and followed Sebastian to the cocktail trolley. "Let me guess," Francois said. "An old-fashioned for Basil and a Manhattan for Sebastian?"

"Ah close, I prefer a mojito," Sebastian said. "But I'll drink whatever."

"Old-fashioned sounds wonderful, thank you." Basil added.

Andrew came in, carrying a large tray of cheese, crackers, salamis and olives, which he set on the sideboard. He looked around, smiling at those assembled. "How's the stay going so far?"

"Very well," Wendla said. "There's ghost children on the lawn."

"I got locked in a secret bookshelf room with Kris," Basil added. He went to join her by the fire. "How're you holding up, by the way?"

"Oh, fine. I spent some time with the scientist there, we… don't really get each other." Kris shrugged and pulled their legs up to their chest. "My room is really cold, like… really, really cold. I'm only just defrosting by the fire."

Basil frowned. "Do you want us to come and try an exorcism on your room? Presence of spirits can manifest like an intense cold."

"If you can exorcise, why don't you do it on the whole house? Right now?" Brit had appeared between them. "I mean, if that's a thing you can do, and you think there's ghosts."

Basil blinked at Brit. "Ah, well, it's actually more complicated than that. I need to know who the ghost is, and why they're haunting the place before I can effectively move them on. It's a conversation, really."

"Huh." Brit didn't roll her eyes but Basil got the idea she wanted to.

Basil glanced past her, hoping that Sebastian would come over and help with the prickly scientist but he was deep in conversation with Wendla. Basil was jealous, still he was the one who'd moved away from Sebastian to talk to Kris.

"So, how's your stay been so far, Brit?" Basil put on his best customer service smile.

She frowned a little. "The food's really good, and my bedroom is comfortable, if a little drafty. Mostly people haven't been interacting with me, I assume because I'm here as the resident skeptic."

"I'm sorry," Basil said. "Sebastian and I would love to interview you, we've got a couple done already, if you have some time maybe tomorrow?"

Brit softened a little. "Yes, I can make time for that."

"Did you get any readings from what you were doing earlier?" Kris asked, a little tentatively.

"Nothing yet on the electromagnetic field reader, and I've had a recording device running all day and I don't think it's picked up anything but the atmospheric noises of the house and people moving around. I'll check the recordings later." She leaned against the back of the armchair. "It all seems somewhat pointless."

"Sebastian uses a lot of the same equipment," Basil said. "You could compare what he's recorded with yours, that's good for scientific experiments right? More data?"

Brit smiled wryly. "Yes, that would be good. Assuming he hasn't tampered with it."

"Oh he would never," Basil felt a bit defensive.

"I'm sure," Brit said. "But I have to take everything into account."

Before Basil could get properly upset and tell Brit to back off, Sebastian himself appeared, a drink in each hand. He gave Basil the shorter of the two glasses. "Wendla and Francois said we can interview them right now, if you're ready?"

Basil's anger deflated and he sipped the drink, it was divine, dry and tart at the same time. "Fine with me. Brit, why don't you take my chair?"

He stood and moved aside for Brit to slide in, and followed Sebastian back towards Wendla. He hadn't even noticed Sebastian shouldering his camera bag on the way down, but there it was. Probably it was just such a normal occurrence now, that Basil didn't even pick up on it.

Brit and Kris turned their chairs to watch as Sebastian set up the camera and gestured for Basil to take over. Basil moved into place and hit record. "Wendla and Francois, sorry I don't think I caught your last name?"

"Bergman," Wendla said.

"Can you tell us a little about yourselves, to start off with?" Sebastian prompted, sipping his mojito.

Basil adjusted the focus a little and smiled as the picture sharpened, he was getting better at this.

"Not much to tell, to be perfectly honest with you. I've always been able to see ghosts, talk to ghouls and suchlike," Wendla said. "I never thought anything of it. I suppose I did some sleuthing and so on as a girl, at school, but once I met Francois we sort of took it on as a consulting business. My parents left a lot of money to me when they died so it doesn't much matter if we don't take many jobs, or if we do pro bono work like this one."

Francois waited for his wife to finish then stepped in. "My friends and I accidentally summoned something, when I was a kid," he said. "It was all fun and games until it showed its fangs, then we really had to work to get rid of it again. I suppose ever since then, I've had a shadow over me, bit of a magnet for the supernatural." He gave Wendla a look of devotion. "But it's how I met my lady love, so I'm not complaining at all."

She leaned in and gave him a brief kiss, the attraction between them palpable. Wendla turned back to the camera with a movie-star smile. Basil was impressed, she was genuinely charismatic in a way not many were. She'd have fans all over the world after Sebastian cut his footage together.

"So, something we've been asking people is where were you when you got the invitation to Beach House?" Sebastian said.

"Oh I don't know," Francois said. "We'd had a fantastic dinner the night before at one of those places in Ponsonby, can't recall the name, but it was absolutely delicious. Had a few too many, caught a cab home. I think we noticed it the next day?"

Wendla shrugged a shoulder. "It was with a few other invites, weddings, dinner parties and gallery openings and so on, we have a very busy social calendar."

Basil could imagine, if he was ever to host a dinner party, he'd love to have the Bergman's attend.

"And what made you decide to take it?"

Francois chuckled. "Who could resist a mysterious house party? And we haven't been disappointed. There was a terrible amount of knocking on the walls last night, from perhaps one to three am? It sounded as if it was inside our wardrobe to begin with, then it moved up and down the internal walls of the room."

"Couldn't make out the purpose," Wendla said. "I asked if anyone wanted to communicate, tried all my usual tricks but it kept on banging away."

"Very strange," Sebastian said. "We didn't hear anything."

"No one else did," Francois said. "That we've been able to ascertain anyway. Wendla said you saw some picnickers this afternoon?"

Sebastian made a note in his notebook. "I need to review my footage, see if any of it showed up, but I haven't quite managed that yet."

"Plenty of time, I'm sure we're going to see far more fireworks tonight." Wendla's bright smile seemed at odds with the promise of more supernatural activity. Behind Basil, Brit snorted.

"It rather puts me in the mind of that gorgeous old house in Florence we stayed at once, maybe in 2010?" Francois said. "Do you remember, Wendla, darling, it was always endlessly banging on the cupboard doors."

"That was a poltergeist," Wendla flapped her hand dismissively. "Completely different vibe to the situation and the manifestation, that one was all malice and misguided violence. Whatever we heard last night, it wanted our attention — although for what it obviously didn't tell us."

"Yes, well —" Sebastian was gearing up for the next question when the parlour door slammed open.

Startled, Basil turned to see Laura-Mae and Randall walking in. Laura-Mae had her usual matching outfit on, something a little more formal than she'd worn at breakfast, but her hair wasn't quite as put together, there were stray hairs flying out of the coiffure and her expression looked tense. Behind her, Randall's good ole boy gregariousness was replaced with tight lips and narrowed eyes.

On seeing everyone turned to look at them, they both forced smiles onto their faces.

Basil glanced back to Sebastian who shook his head and said "cut." He turned to Wendla and Francois and thanked them for the interview.

Basil turned off the camera and stowed it away. "How was your day?" Brit asked Laura-Mae, they were both at the cheeseboard now.

Randall took Brit's empty seat and sat with his head propped on one hand. Kris eyed him and then went back to her novel.

Basil went to join them for some cheese.

"Oh, it was, yes, very very eventful," Laura-Mae said. "We picked up an awful lot of vibrations outside this morning?"

Basil helped himself to a slice of brie. "Whereabouts outside?"

"Oh in the chapel, of course," Laura-Mae said. "Very evil sort of place, that. My theory is that a priest was put to death by Satanists there."

"That's strange," Basil said. "From what Sebastian said the chapel was the one place in the whole estate he felt completely comfortable."

Brit looked up sharply, watching Laura-Mae's face.

Laura-Mae frowned and sliced a bit of quince paste with rather more force than necessary. "Well, I don't wish to cast aspersions, Sebastian is a very nice boy, but I know what I felt."

"Do you have any evidence of the satanist angle?" Brit asked, her mouth pulling into a smile. "Perhaps you found some pentacles, or strange writings?"

Laura-Mae looked between them, her eyelids flicking quickly. "Yes, there was, now that you mention it, I did see a pentacle or two."

"Strange indeed," Basil said, as soothingly as he could manage. He was willing to at least give her the appearance of giving the benefit of the doubt.

"Perhaps we should take a look together after dinner?" Brit suggested. "I certainly haven't seen anything definitive."

"Yes," Laura-Mae nodded emphatically. "Let's all go over together this evening." She took a bit of her cracker and chewed quickly. "How did you fare today, Basil?"

"Very eventful day," he said, borrowing Laura-Mae's phrasing. "But I don't want to rehash it all now and then again at dinner, I'm sure Horatio will want an update from all of us."

"Of course. If you'll excuse me, I just realised I forgot something important in the car," Laura-Mae said.

Basil and Brit watched as she crossed the room, got a bunch of car keys off Randall and exited towards the front door.

"What do you think she forgot in her car?" Basil asked softly, biting back a smile.

"I think, almost certainly, she forgot to carve some pentacles into a bit of the chapel," Brit said.

"What about the chapel?" Sebastian snatched a piece of brie from Basil and popped it in his mouth.

"Rude," Basil said, cutting himself another slice. "We are merely speculating that Laura-Mae might be able to vandalise it in order to support her story."

"Hard luck," Sebastian said. "Pretty sure Horatio locks it overnight, and the sun is going down."

Brit laughed then, although not in a mean way, she sounded genuinely amused. "You two are the most down to earth out of all the kooks here."

"Thank you, I think." Basil chuckled and fed Sebastian a piece of aged cheddar.

Laura-Mae came back in shortly afterwards, her cheeks flushed and her expression displeased.

"Found what you wanted?" Brit teased.

Laura-Mae gave a tight-lipped smile and sat beside her husband, perching on the arm of the chair and murmuring to him softly.

There was a knock on the door to the parlour. "It's open," Basil said.

The door remained closed.

The knocking continued. It grew steadily louder.

"This is ridiculous," Brit said. "Just because the Bergmans were talking about weird knocking." She strode to the door and pulled it open. There was no one on the other side.

Brit leaned out, but when she stood back her face was pale. "There's no one there, no one at all." She looked up, and all around, perhaps searching for a mechanism or something to explain the sound. "Nothing."

Basil beckoned her back, feeling the familiar prickle of supernatural activity. Brit returned to his side, letting the door swing shut behind her.

The banging resumed the moment the door clicked shut.

"I don't understand," Brit's voice had turned hoarse. She walked backwards, eyes fixed on the door. "Perhaps there's something embedded in the door itself?"

As if in response, the banging moved, up over the frame of the door until it seemed the wall above would shake from the force of it.

Bam! Bam! Bam!

Sebastian fumbled his camera out and started filming.

"It's moving," Laura-Mae whimpered. Basil glanced back to see her clinging to Randall, genuinely frightened.

Basil moved towards the sound, Kris stood beside him. "It's all right," Basil said. "It's only a sound, it can't hurt us."

The knocking moved to the ceiling. A deeper booming noise now.

Brit gasped.

Wendla tutted. "Who's there? Show yourself! Enough of this nonsense. You must have heard me talking and decided to play this little prank, so out you come." Her tone was imperious, commanding and her voice carried easily.

The knocking ceased.

Basil summoned up a little of his magic, using it to reach out to whatever it was. He could feel something, just out of reach... then it was gone.

"Well," Francois said. "They didn't like you talking to them like that, did they?" He patted Wendla on the shoulder. "Good work, love."

"No doubt it'll be back," she said, and downed the last of her drink.

The door to the dining room slammed open and everyone jumped, turning to stare. Horatio stood there, blinking back at them all, Eve right behind them. "Uh, dinner is ready? What happened in here?"

Brit burst out laughing. "Oh nothing, just someone knocking on the ceiling with a battering ram!"

"Oh dear," Kris moved closer to Brit and gently took her elbow. "That might have broken her."

Brit shook her head, giggling uncontrollably.

Sebastian lowered his camera. "We all heard something and, uh, it was a lot."

"That... sounds about right." Horatio held the door open and they all filtered past to sit at the dining table.

Laura-Mae was white as a sheet, and Randall looked like he'd eaten some very bad fish — green around the gills. Whatever they'd claimed to be, Sebastian would bet cash money that Laura-Mae and Randall had never seen actual paranormal activity before, and they didn't know how to cope.

CHAPTER TEN

SEBASTIAN

The mood at dinner quickly turned festive. Most of the guests were shaken by the knocking, but after a while, the nervousness turned to excitement.

They'd all been there to witness it, after all. The house was definitely haunted (even if Brit couldn't quite admit it yet), and there was the feeling of having had a shared adventure. The camaraderie grew when the food was brought out.

Eve had made an extravagant Italian dinner — various forms of pasta, including vegetarian lasagne, chicken and mushroom cream fettuccine, cheese ravioli and fresh spaghetti tossed with garlic and olive oil.

"Eve, this is amazing,"

Sebastian and Basil tucked in with hearty appetites. "Is this pasta made fresh?" Basil asked, turning to Andrew as he took his spot down the table.

"Yes, this afternoon," he replied.

"It's wonderful."

While they ate, Wendla regaled Horatio with the story of the knocking in the parlour.

Horatio's eyes widened. "Sounds like the knocking I used to hear in my rooms, upstairs. I've never heard it downstairs, though."

"All us magic-type people in the house," Kris said. "It's waking things up."

Sebastian shivered delicately. "Don't love that phrasing."

"It's true though," Basil said, his voice soft, almost apologetic. "I can feel it too. As if the house itself is somehow aware of us."

"Excuse me," Laura-Mae said. She had stood up, and her chair squeaked on the floor as she shoved it back. "I'm not feeling entirely well. I'm going to go and lie down." She swept out of the room without looking at the others.

Randall cleared his throat and took a last bite of lasagne and stood as well. "I'd better go and take care of her."

Sebastian did his best to forget what Basil had said about the house being aware. He watched Randall walk out.

Once they'd left, Sebastian turned to Horatio. "Is the chapel locked?"

Horatio nodded. "Yes, I locked it mid afternoon, when I came back inside."

Basil breathed a sigh of relief. "That's something, it should all be intact then."

"Unless Laura-Mae has some lockpicking skills neither of us guessed," Sebastian added.

Horatio raised their eyebrows. "I'm very much regretting inviting the Rhodeses."

"Everyone makes mistakes, dear," Wendla said. "And not everyone is as fabulous as those of us now present."

Sebastian chuckled and Horatio did the same after a moment.

Beside him, Basil tensed. Sebastian glanced at him. "Something wrong?"

"A presence," Basil said. "I can't tell if it's the same as before or if it's something, someone else..."

Francois sniffed, as if scenting the air. "Yes, I feel it too."

Kris pushed their chair back, one of their bracelets lighting up as they looked around.

"What should we do?" Horatio signalled to the staff to be alert, although they were all paying attention anyway.

"Please stay put," Basil said. "I sense an intention but I'm not sure—" Basil's speech cut off abruptly. His body stiffened, even more upright than usual. His eyes widened, then rolled back.

"Basil!" Sebastian grabbed for Basil's hands, they were icy cold.

Kris moved closer. "I don't know if it's a good idea to touch him," they said. "Sebastian, maybe—"

"So cold," Basil said. The voice that came out of him was undoubtedly his, but it was softer, frailer somehow, perhaps the voice of a younger person? "I'm so cold."

Sebastian's skin broke into goosebumps and he shivered. "Basil?"

Basil's eyes rolled forward, but they weren't his usual blue. They were a rich, chocolate brown. Sebastian gripped Basil's hands tighter. "Basil?"

"That's a plant," Basil said, in that strange voice.

"What's going on?" Brit asked. "Why is he talking like that?"

"It's been so long, so long in the cold and the dark. No one heard me scream," Basil intoned. His voice pitched higher.

"He's possessed," Kris said. They picked up a knife and started hacking at one of the patches on their overalls.

Sebastian jolted, Kris was about to rescue Basil, but that meant they only had a short amount of time to question whatever spirit was inside him. He leaned forward, peering into Basil's face. "What's your name?"

"Name? I lay on the soil when he cast me out, I thought that would be an end of it. But his plans were worse than that, worse indeed." Basil laughed, an uncanny high-pitched giggle that Sebastian never wanted to hear, ever again.

"What did he do? Can you tell us?"

"They left me alone with him, they promised they wouldn't." Basil's hands gripped Sebastian's painfully tight. Sebastian had the impression Basil's hands were somehow smaller, more wiry, than normal. Could possession affect the physical? Well, it had already affected his eyes hadn't it?

Kris made an 'ah ha!' noise of success as the patch came loose from their overalls. It was a star-shaped embroidered patch. Sebastian gave them a look, hoping they'd pick up on what he was doing. Kris set down the knife and hesitated before moving closer again.

"I have to do it soon, Sebastian," they hissed.

"He... he..." Basil began to cry, sobbing like a small child.

Sebastian nearly pulled away then. The tears streaming from Basil's eyes were dark, brackish water, and the smell of them filled the room — like rotting leaves and damp left for far too long. His love for Basil overcame the need to escape though, and he held steady.

Basil's sobs turned into shrieks.

Sebastian gripped his hands tight. "Kris, do it!"

Kris spoke some arcane words that prickled in Sebastian's ears like static, and then placed the torn off patch on Basil's shoulder.

The noise of the shrieking stopped instantly, and Basil slumped in a swoon. Sebastian pushed closer, catching Basil with his arms and his body so he didn't hit his head on the table. Then they both sort of slithered to the floor.

"What. The fuck. Was that?" Brit's voice wasn't the usual calm and collected tone.

Horatio knelt beside Basil and Sebastian, helping to move Basil into the recovery position. The front of his sweater was soaked, and the water had spilled over the table and floor as well. Horatio knelt in a puddle of it. "How can I help?"

Kris crouched on their other side. "He should be fine in a moment, possessions take it out of you though."

"Is... is the ghost still here, could it try one of us next?" Horatio asked.

Kris shook their head. "It'll be around somewhere, but banishing it the way I did will push it back for a while at least. I'll... make patches for all of you, to stop this happening again."

Sebastian was vaguely aware of the sounds of Francois and Wendla soothing Brit, but he kept his gaze focused on Basil.

"When will he wake up?"

"I'm not sure..." Kris said. "I'm sorry, he's a witch, it probably makes a difference. The people I've seen possessed before have been regular humans."

Sebastian nodded some. "Perhaps we should get him to bed, then. Could you help me with him? I can lift him all right but getting up the stairs might be precarious."

"Of course."

Sebastian scooped Basil into his arms and lifted him. Kris moved chairs and things, making a clear path to the door.

"I can help, son," Francois said, following close at Sebastian's elbow.

Brit had her head in her hands, shoulders shaking. Wendla rubbed circles on her back with one hand, and offered a drink with her other.

Between the three of them, they got Basil safely to the Blue Room and laid on the bed. Sebastian removed his shoes, and tugged his soaked clothes off his torso, pulling the blankets over him. Once that was done, he stood and looked at his helpers.

"Thank you, for everything," Sebastian hugged Kris, desperate for a warm human touch.

Surprised, they hugged him back. "Of course. You keep hold of that patch, I can make more right now, for the others. Do you want me to stay?"

"Yes, please," Sebastian said. "You too, Francois, if you don't mind. I don't particularly want to be alone until he wakes."

"Of course, I think I see some brandy on the sideboard, I daresay we could all use some of that." He went to pour some glasses.

"What was that?" Basil's voice was scratchy and weak, but it was his again.

Sebastian sat down beside him on the bed and took his hand. It wasn't nearly as cold as it'd been before. "Thank the earth mother. How are you feeling?"

"Why am I in bed?" Basil went to sit up and then moaned, falling back down.

"Try not to move too much," Kris said. "You were possessed, I had to boot the thing out of you. You'll be woozy and weak for a few hours yet."

Basil made a surprised noise, and settled on the pillows. "Oh. Well, thank you Kris."

Francois appeared on the other side of the bed and pressed a small glass of brandy into Sebastian's hand. "See if you can get that in him, should bolster him up."

"Maybe some more food, too," Kris tidied Basil's discarded shoes out of the way. "I'll bring something up from the dining room. Basil, I don't think you should get up aside from using the bathroom. Get a good night's sleep."

Basil nodded, as Sebastian held the glass to his lips and he sipped.

"Thank you," Sebastian said. "I don't want to leave him."

The evening was a short one after that. Sebastian helped Basil change into his pajamas. Basil used the bathroom and washed his face. He ate some of the bread and butter Kris brought up. Horatio dropped by to deliver some chamomile tea and to apologise.

Sebastian helped Basil get comfortable in bed, making sure he was warm enough by adding another blanket. Basil fell asleep soon after he was comfortable, and although he was worried, and not a bit spooked, Sebastian drifted off soon after.

CHAPTER ELEVEN

BASIL

B asil woke around eight in the morning feeling his normal self, which was a relief after the night before. He couldn't recall what had happened at dinner, from what Sebastian and Kris had said he'd been possessed. But by who? And for what reason?

Sebastian was still snoring lightly, so Basil eased out of bed and went for a shower, considering.

If a spirit had gone to the trouble of possession, it must have had an important message to share.

He stepped out of the shower and dried off, then shaved his face. He had to check out the chapel, that felt important to him somehow. And there was something else, something he couldn't remember, but was niggling at the edge of his brain.

He'd have to ask the others what he'd said when he was possessed.

When he emerged from the en suite, Sebastian was sitting up, his expression worried. "How're you feeling?"

"Much better, normal," Basil said. "You?"

Sebastian stretched his arms over his head. "Yeah, slept fine, which seems impossible given everything that happened yesterday."

"Exhaustion," Basil sat by Sebastian and rubbed his knee where it was tenting the blanket. "That must have been terrifying to witness. Are you okay?"

Sebastian frowned but nodded. "Yeah, Kris was amazing, Horatio and the Bergmans too. We've got to get to the bottom of this though, I don't want to risk anything like that happening again. Kris gave us this patch for clothes." There was a star-shaped embroidered patch on the mattress, and he pressed it to Basil's hand. "Put it in your pocket or something, okay?"

Basil took the patch and slipped it into his pants pocket, pulling them on. "I agree about needing to solve this mystery. Let's go have a big breakfast and investigate for real."

Breakfast was quiet, only Kris and Horatio were at the table. Horatio looked up and half-stood when Basil and Sebastian came in.

"Feeling better?" they asked.

"Great, honestly," Basil said. "Thank you for looking after me last night, both of you."

Horatio sat down again.

Kris was multitasking, eating breakfast and sewing something small with a needle and thread. "Glad to hear it, slept well did you?"

"Very well," Basil helped himself to eggs, bacon and a small bowl of hot porridge out of a slow cooker on the buffet. "Thanks."

"Laura-Mae and Randall left," Horatio said. "Didn't even say goodbye, just snuck out in the night."

"No way." Sebastian had loaded a plate with toast and eggs and took a seat beside Kris. "Guess they couldn't handle the haunting?"

"Seems like it," Horatio said.

Kris snorted. "They were used to being the only experts, with everyone else in awe of them. Must have been a shock to be in here with all of us, and a real haunting."

"Probably for the best," Sebastian said. "I don't think they'd have been any help with actually solving anything."

Kris sipped their coffee. "Can't say I'll miss them."

"Are Wendla and Francois here still?" Basil asked. He didn't think they were the type to flee in the night, but you never quite knew.

"Their car is still in the drive," Horatio said. "And their door is closed, I assume they're just sleeping in."

"I heard some movement in the hallways in the early hours," Kris said. "I didn't sense spirits and there was no more knocking, so maybe it was them doing some sleuthing?"

"Could be." Basil dug into his breakfast, sighing some at how delicious it was.

After a few minutes of companionable silence, Kris leaned over and handed the thing they'd been working on to Sebastian. It was a hand sewn shooting star, with a silvery tail, the star itself made of soft oranges and yellows. "This is for you. Put it in your pocket or pin it on, it's a ward against possession."

Basil felt the patch that Kris had given him last night, it was safe in his trouser pocket. "Thank you, Kris," he said.

"I'm making them for everyone," Kris said.

Horatio pointed to a purple and blue star on their chest, pinned on proudly. "I got mine already."

"It's no problem," Kris smiled and shook their head. "I like doing it, and it's easy for me. I don't know if it's entirely foolproof, the spirits here are kinda unpredictable."

"On that note, is the chapel open this morning?" Sebastian asked.

"Yes, I opened it before breakfast. No signs of any tampering with anything. You're welcome to use it, film, whatever. I trust you all."

"Do you want to come with us?" Basil asked Kris. "I'd like to check out the chapel and head back to the library as well, anywhere else we know has had activity."

"The parlour," Kris suggested, nodding at the connecting door. "This room?"

"I wonder if the parlour is a place of interest, or if we had activity here and in there simply because we were all gathered there... the spirits could have been responding to the presences." Basil dabbed at his mouth with a linen napkin.

"We should film in all of them," Sebastian said. "I'll get my EMF reader, maybe the spirit box."

Kris chuckled. "I'm happy to accompany you but I can't guarantee that my magic won't put your electronics on the fritz."

"Maybe I'll leave them in the bedroom..." Sebastian said, easy-going as ever. "Brit, is she all right? She was upset last night."

Horatio nodded. "She asked Andrew if she could have breakfast in her room this morning, I think she's taking some time to process."

"Very fair."

Basil stacked his empty plate with Sebastian's. His urgency hadn't faded, and he was eager to get things started.

They went back to their respective rooms and met in the foyer of the Manor.

"We'll start with the chapel," Basil suggested. "I want to see it, and I have a sort of hunch that there's something to find there."

Kris had pulled on a pair of brightly coloured boots and an over-the-shoulder sling bag.

Sebastian had his camera but had left his other tools and devices in the bedroom.

Basil had brought some crystals. He'd picked up his tarot cards, then put them down again. If they couldn't find any answers by sundown, he might do some readings in different rooms. It could give valuable insight that snooping around physically might not.

But that was for later.

Now, Sebastian led the way down the path towards the side of the house. Basil could feel the autumn chill, and see dew on the grass and plants that were still in the shadow of the house and trees. The air was clear and crisp, and Basil took deep breaths, enjoying the way it felt in his lungs.

The morning was sunny, but there were a number of clouds in the sky. Some of them looked heavy, dark grey with the promise of rain. Basil could easily imagine how it would feel to be stuck in the haunted house at night with torrential rain pouring down outside.

If it wasn't for the ghost, it'd be a very pleasant sensation.

All the more reason to solve the mystery as soon as possible.

Sebastian had reached the chapel but he hadn't gone in. He was looking at it critically from the outside. Basil hurried to catch up.

"What is it?" Basil asked, his voice low and gentle, sure Sebastian had noticed something and wanting to draw it out.

"I think... the inside doesn't quite match the outside," Sebastian said. He passed Basil his camera, his expression serious. "Film me, will you?"

Basil shouldered the camera, he was practically an expert at it by now, and set it recording. He gave Sebastian a thumbs up.

Sebastian paced from corner to corner of the chapel, counting his steps. First the front, then up the side. He came back to Basil. "The back wall has a stained glass window but I think the chapel inside isn't as wide as it is outside."

"Oooh," Kris said. "Hidden room?"

"I don't think it's large enough to be called a whole room, but I think there might be a false wall, maybe?"

"Let's go in and find out," Kris opened the chapel door.

Sebastian followed and Basil came last, pausing in the door to take a sweeping shot of the inside of the chapel. This place had a very different vibe to the Manor. Basil could feel a deep, enduring sense of peace. If buildings had auras, he'd see soft golden light in the chapel. He instantly understood why Sebastian had relaxed here.

He swung the camera around, focused on Sebastian as he paced the room, counting aloud.

"This is the outside wall," Kris said, knocking on the wall to the right. "It sounds solid."

Sebastian knocked on the wall to the left. "Hollow," he said. His face lit up.

"What is with this place?" Basil murmured.

"The question is, how do we open it?" Kris hurried to the other end of the left wall and knocked as well. "I don't see anything."

"There will be some hidden latch or button..." Sebastian mused. He moved up the wall, both hands roaming over it. Kris did the same from the other end.

There was a loud *chunk* and Kris sprang back as a section of the wall shifted outwards, protruding just a touch. "Found it."

Basil moved closer, staying at the end of the bench seating in the centre of the chapel so as to record a wide view.

Sebastian and Kris each took one side of what seemed to be a removable panel, and pulled it free of the wall. Laying it against one of the benches they looked inside.

It revealed a dim passageway, barely three feet deep.

Sebastian didn't hesitate, he stepped in, then reached back. "Basil, can I have the camera please?"

Basil's heart fluttered — Sebastian was polite even when he was clearly excited about a new discovery. Basil passed the camera over. Kris took a cautious step back. Whatever it was about mages that screwed with technology, they weren't taking any risks.

"Thank you." Sebastian moved further into the wall.

Basil knew he ought to be worried, there was something strange going on, and the day before he and Kris had been trapped in a hidden room, but it was impossible to feel worried about the chapel. It was too calm and blessed of a place. Sacred, no matter what your personal beliefs were.

Kris didn't follow Sebastian in, they caught Basil's eye. "I know we removed the panel, but I'm still not going in there. You can, I'll stand guard."

"Fair enough," Basil said. He followed Sebastian.

The passage in the wall was unfinished, unpainted plasterboard and very, very dusty. Sebastian had crab-walked down it some ways.

"Can you see anything?"

"Books," Sebastian said.

Basil's heart leapt. He loved when the investigation led them to books. He wondered what they'd find this time...Perhaps the missing family tree page, torn out of the bible?

He turned and looked up the other direction, summoning a glowing orb in one hand to light his way. Then, thinking again, he summoned another and sent it down over Sebastian's head so he could see a little more.

"Thanks, Basil," Sebastian said. Basil edged his way up the other end of the passage way. He didn't love how close the walls were, and he couldn't help the fear of being trapped there that flared up in his mind, but he kept moving. Perhaps there were more books?

His light didn't show any items on the floor. Looking up there were patches of wall that had been drawn on, though. He paused, gesturing for the light to come in closer so he could see what it was.

The drawings were of charcoal, crude scribbles, which all seemed to be of holes, or the letter O. He frowned. "Strange drawings here," he said, raising his voice so everyone could hear. "Lots of holes or Os or something."

"You'll want to see these books," Sebastian said.

Basil backed up, eager to be out of the wall so he could examine Sebastian's findings.

He stepped back into the chapel with a sigh of relief.

Kris's face broke into a smile. "Thank goodness, I don't know what I'd have done if you'd got stuck."

Sebastian edged out a moment later, one hand holding his camera, the other arm loaded with books. He was covered in dust, and Basil guessed he must look the same. He dusted off his shoulders then took the books from Sebastian, retreating to sit on one of the benches to look them over.

Kris moved to stand behind Basil, to read over his shoulder.

Sebastian, grinning, adjusted the camera to film them both.

"This one's a hymnal," Basil said. He flipped through it. "Seems perfectly normal, although the age on it means it's relatively valuable."

He set it aside and picked up the next, a larger book with no title on it. Inside it was full of handwriting, a heavy, precise hand that indicated a scholar who was used to recording their thoughts.

"It's a journal I think," Basil said. "The first date is 1897." He scanned the pages, skim reading. "Written by a priest."

"How about that?" Kris said. "I wonder if there's any scandalous secrets in there?"

"I feel like there must be, otherwise why hide it like this?"

"What are the other books?"

Reluctantly, Basil closed the journal, but he kept it on his lap as he picked up the others. "A copy of Dante's *Inferno*, I can see why he hid this one." He chuckled. "And another hymnal. I wonder... perhaps the hymnals are hiding something I can't immediately see, but I think the journal is the real treasure here."

"Maybe he hid the hymnals with the others to obscure the journal?" Kris suggested.

"Could be." Basil set them aside and opened up the journal again. "I'd like to read this, Sebastian, I think it needs studying."

Sebastian shut off the camera. "I agree. You do that, are you comfortable here?"

"Very." Basil usually would want more cushioning in his chair, and a cup of tea, but the chapel was such a pleasant environment he didn't care at all.

Kris and Sebastian replaced the panel in the wall and left him to it.

Basil started reading in earnest.

The accounts started ordinarily enough, reports of sermons given to the family and the servants, and then how the neighbours had started to attend as well. The family seemed to be Catholic, but there was some mention that Edmund welcomed locals of all Christian faiths, which seemed very ahead of his time. Maybe it was simply the rural setting that necessitated it?

Basil ascertained the priest was one of the children of Lord Crane, who had built the Manor house and settled there with his family after shipping over from England.

There was no record of the priest's name, he hadn't written it in the front of the journal and of course, he didn't refer to himself by name. There was mention of two younger sisters though, Antonia and Layla. Antonia lived nearby with her husband but visited often, and Layla seemed to be something of a black sheep. Although the priest spoke of her very fondly, it seemed she was always in trouble with their father.

The priest mentioned a frequent visitor to the Manor as well, an unpleasant man who visited for weeks at a time and had his father's ear. The priest described him as an unsettling presence, who he noted often stared at Layla when he thought no one was looking.

The priest didn't name this strange gentleman, but described him as 'the tall man in the grey suit' or more often 'the odious visitor'.

Basil licked his lips, wondering if this odious man had something to do with why the house was haunted. Could he be a visiting serial killer? Who worked his way through the family?

Then Basil turned a journal page and startled, almost throwing the book aside.

Heart racing, he forced himself to look at the page. It was a charcoal drawing of the man himself. It was crude, not a very precise drawing, but something about the eyes was horribly familiar. The priest had titled the drawing *Asher Sinclair* and signed it with his name, Edmund Crane.

Asher.

The same Asher?

It had to be. Asher said he'd been killing witches to gain long life after all, so this was one of the places he must have been, way back in the day.

Basil shivered lightly, half-convinced that the real Asher could somehow be looking at him through those charcoal eyes. He turned the page.

"All right, Edmund, what else did you notice?"

The journal updates became less frequent. Attendance at the chapel services dwindled, and it seemed Asher had moved in, installed himself as a permanent fixture.

Edmund reported being afraid for Layla's safety, and then his own.

Basil found a daisy chain, pressed between the pages and very lightly brushed his finger over it. It was Layla's work, he knew. He wondered how things had ended... was she the witch Asher had wanted? Was Edmund? Back in the day, many people with magical gifts had hidden them, or simply never properly awoken them. A spiritual man like Edmund could easily have been one such case.

Edmund described a picnic the siblings and their friends shared on the lawn, and how Layla had made him a daisy chain. Basil smiled to himself.

Apparently the picnic had been fun but had ended with their father Hugh, storming through in a rage, shouting at them, although what he had shouted, Edmund hadn't been able to understand.

Edmund's next lines were hurried, the handwriting less neat, as he confessed that things had gone wrong, and he didn't trust he had a future.

Basil read the last sentences aloud. *"I must protect my sister. I shall stow this record where none shall find it, because none but me know of the extra work the carpenters did on this chapel. I shall do what I can, but I fear that Asher has corrupted my father beyond saving. I am not long for this world. May Mother Mary save us."*

There were no more entries, only blank pages after that.

A soft shiver when through Basil's body and he closed his eyes. "Wherever you are, Edmund, I'm sorry, and we'll do our best to send your family to rest," he promised.

A rush of warmth enveloped him. It felt very much like a thank you.

CHAPTER TWELVE

SEBASTIAN

S ebastian and Kris met Brit on the path back to the Manor.

"Good morning," Brit said. "Do you mind if I walk with you?" She wore a thick, handmade woollen cardigan in bright forest green, and it was wrapped tightly around her. From the bags under her eyes, Sebastian guessed she hadn't slept much.

"Of course," Sebastian said. "How are you, Brit?"

Brit shook her head. "I don't want to talk about it, I just..." She shook her head again.

Sebastian understood on a deep, visceral level.

The three of them walked in silence, making their slow way back into the Manor house, breathing the fresh, cool air and listening to the birdsong and the crunch of their feet on the path.

"Where to now?" Kris asked.

"Let's start in the parlour," Sebastian said.

Brit bit her lip but followed along. "What are you going to do?"

"See if we can't get some film evidence of the haunting," Sebastian said. "I should have grabbed a ouija board when I was packing."

"We can make our own easily enough," Kris said. "But honestly? I don't think we'll need it. We can call out to them."

Brit sat close to the fire, arms wrapped around herself and watched.

Kris went to the shelves and pulled out an ancient Scrabble box, tipping the tiles out on a coffee table and flipping them so the letters were right side up.

Sebastian filmed as the door slammed itself shut again. Kris looked up at the top of the doorframe. "Well? We're here, come talk to us! I know you can hear me!"

The knocking came almost the instant Kris stopped speaking. Loud, resounding thumps like a giant knocking on the other side of the wall.

Sebastian's breath caught. "They were ready."

Kris nodded. "Yes, they were. Listen to me, we can't tell much from the knocking but there are letters on the table. How about you use them to spell out your names?"

The knocking ceased. Sebastian, hopeful, turned the camera to focus on the Scrabble tiles, but there was no movement.

Brit gasped, and huddled further into the armchair. "It's cold. Can you hear that?" Sebastian opened his mouth to ask what but then the sound of crying came to his ears as well.

Kris caught his eye and grimaced. "That's new."

It sounded like a woman, crying as if there was nothing left to live for. Sebastian shivered, and pressed his hand over the shooting star patch Kris had made him. He panned the camera slowly around the room, there was a sort of shimmering happening next to the table of Scrabble tiles.

He kept the camera on it, but gestured for Kris to look.

Kris saw instantly and murmured something softly, rubbing their fingers on one of the woven bracelets on their wrist.

Slowly the tiles moved, rearranging themselves.

"Oh, I hate that," Brit moaned. "Who's doing that?"

The tiles stopped moving, then slowly started again, spelling out the words *Layla Crane*.

Sebastian watched, eyes flicking from the table to the viewfinder of his camera, trying to see something in the shimmer the camera was picking up.

He cleared his throat. "Layla Crane? You used to live here, didn't you?"

In the camera the shimmer resolved into a figure, a young woman, probably no more than eighteen, in a long dress, her hair pulled up into a strict chignon.

She was bent over the table, moving the tiles. Sebastian's breath caught. "I can see her, in the camera."

Brit's breathing was rasping, too fast. It sounded like she might be having a panic attack.

He had to help her, but Layla was spelling out something else.

He moved closer, to get a better shot, as Layla arranged the tiles to spell the words *Attic* and then *Asher S.*

"Asher?" Sebastian dropped the camera, his voice far louder than it should have been. The movement and the noise seemed to break the spell, as Layla vanished instantly.

Kris had moved to Brit's side and slipped an arm around her. Sebastian picked up his camera with shaking hands and turned it off, then went to crouch in front of Brit.

Brit had her arms tight around herself, rocking back and forth. "I can't," she rasped. "I can't, I can't, I can't."

"Brit, it's all right," Kris said. "The ghost has gone, you could go home too if you wanted, like the Rhodes's did."

Brit shook her head. "I can't!"

Sebastian exchanged a look with Kris and tried a different tack. "Brit, you're a scientist aren't you? That means you make a hypothesis and you try to prove it. You gather evidence, isn't that right?"

Kris rubbed wide circles on Brit's back. "That's the scientific method, right?"

Brit managed a nod.

"So look at it this way, you've just seen some evidence you didn't expect, but it's all part of the same experiment. It's new data, that's all."

Brit took a long, shuddering breath and sat up a little straighter, her arms loosening. "New data?"

"Yes, and what do you do with new data?" Sebastian tried his best to coach her, without being condescending. "When it's me, I review the footage and make notes."

Brit huffed in another breath and pushed her shoulders back. She met Sebastian's gaze, her eyes red and teary. "Make notes, analyze the data."

"Great, yes," Sebastian said. "So, that's what you do next and that's how you process what's going on."

Brit slumped back in the armchair and closed her eyes. "Yes, data points. It was data I never expected to find but that doesn't mean anything. Magellan never meant to discover a passage through to the Pacific Ocean, but he did."

"He sure did," Kris said.

Brit took another breath. "Thank you, both of you, that's never happened to me before."

"Seeing a ghost?" Sebastian asked.

"Panic attack, I'm assuming that's what it was," Brit sat up, adjusting her cardigan. "Highly unpleasant."

"I think so, yes," Sebastian said. "Take care of yourself now. Do you want a cup of tea?"

"Yes please, two sugars."

The sideboard always had tea things out, so Sebastian busied himself making her tea and watching out the corner of his eye.

"Here, take this," Kris said. They pressed a pink star cluster embroidered patch into Brit's hand. "It'll keep you safe. I made it, it has protection magic in it."

Brit's hand closed around the patch and she jutted her chin out. "Thank you. I'm not sure I've had sufficient proof of magic yet, but I appreciate the gesture."

Kris smiled easily. "Please, keep it on you, okay?"

"I will, thanks." Brit looked more herself when Sebastian handed her the cup of tea, a piece of shortbread on the saucer. "Thanks to both of you."

"Any time," Sebastian said. "We'll leave you to it, I'd like to get back to Basil now."

Brit nodded as he picked up his camera and walked out with Kris. Once they were out in the fresh air Sebastian relaxed a little.

"You reacted when she spelled out that name, Asher," Kris said. "Why?"

"We... well, Basil and I had a run in with a man named Asher, he was a mage, but not... not like you are. He's very evil, and he got away."

"But Layla couldn't have known the same man, surely," Kris said. "It'd have to be a coincidence."

"He was draining other people's power to stay young," Sebastian glanced around the gardens. There was no way Asher could pop out from behind the rose bushes, but he was nervous all the same.

They passed the lawn where the picnickers had been and Sebastian saw the flicker of movement. He grasped Kris's arm. "There!"

Kris looked and they both watched as a tableau of young people, dressed as Layla had been, in vintage fashion, appeared on a blanket on the lawn.

But their faces weren't smiling and happy, and there was something wrong with their eyes. "What...?"

First one, then more of the figures turned their faces towards Kris and Sebastian. Their eyes were gone. Instead large black holes gaped in their faces. One of the women opened her mouth and black water gushed out.

Sebastian heard buzzing in his eyes and spots formed in his vision. He wasn't breathing, he couldn't breathe.

"Run!" Kris took his hand in a vice-like grip and yanked so hard his shoulder was in danger of dislocating.

Sebastian ran, barely able to process what was happening.

"Don't look back!"

Sebastian realised his neck had been swivelling. He didn't *want* to look back, but he was about to all the same. He bit his tongue and focused his gaze on Kris's back.

His legs moved in a way that felt totally unnatural as he was hauled along, so fast, he could barely keep his feet.

They arrived at the chapel and crashed inside, Kris slamming the door behind them.

Basil looked up, surprised. "What happened?"

Kris shoved Sebastian into the nearest pew. "Sebastian?"

Sebastian's throat worked, he wanted to say something but he couldn't. His chest ached, struggling to take a breath. He closed his eyes, wanting to give in to the abyss.

Someone took his hands. He felt warmth.

Life-giving warmth.

"Where's his patch?" Kris asked from some distance away. He felt hands patting his chest and then pressing down.

More warmth.

Purple sparkles surrounded him. From the darkness he'd sunken into, he saw the purple of Basil's love, Basil's magic, forming a lifeline. He took it eagerly, he trusted Basil. Basil would never hurt him.

Golden light interwove with Basil's purple, and then a striking crimson as well. Sebastian took a breath. It hurt, it ached like his lungs were sick, or full of water, but he took it and shuddering, breathed it out again.

He opened his eyes to see Basil wreathed in a familiar purple glow.

His Basil.

"Basil," he said. His chest eased and he squeezed Basil's hands.

Basil's eyes flew open and he let go of Sebastian's hands to throw his arms around him. "My love."

Kris hugged them both, Sebastian could feel them trembling a little as well.

"What is going on?" Kris sighed, squeezing and then letting go.

"It's ramping up," Sebastian said. "We saw a ghost, her name was Layla Crane."

Basil sat back on his heels, his hand taking Sebastian's again. "Layla was the youngest Crane sibling," Basil said. "The journal told me almost everything I needed to know. She was being targeted, I think, by her father and by a visitor to the house."

"A visitor," Sebastian said.

In the same moment Sebastian and Basil both said. "Asher was here."

Kris shuddered. "Okay you two, never speak at the same time again. That was well creepy and we just saw a haunted picnic outside."

Sebastian, despite it all, chuckled. "Got it. No more speaking in unison."

"I believe Asher was here, feeding on Layla Crane, possibly the other children. I think he's to blame for whatever happened to them." Sebastian's head cleared slowly. He felt like he'd surfaced from some deep, dark place. "How do we help them?"

"How did you know Asher was here?" Basil asked.

"Makeshift ouija board," Kris said. "Layla spelled out her name and Asher."

Sebastian grabbed at Basil's shirt. "She spelled attic as well. We haven't been to the attic at all."

"I thought Horatio said it wasn't safe," Basil said.

"They did," Kris said. "They said it was unsound or something. But if we let them know that's where we need to go?"

"We can't just barrel up there with no plan," Basil said. "We don't even know what happened to Bastian."

"A near-possession," Kris said. "I think."

"I felt like I couldn't breathe," Sebastian said. "Cold, and dark, like you said last night, Basil when it had you."

There was silence for a moment.

"Well the attic's our best bet, it's the only place a ghost has explicitly told us about," Basil said. "We'll gather up Wendla and Francois, Horatio and Brit if they want to come. We'll all bring our things, my crystals and cards, Kris's threads, anything we need, and we can head up to the attic together as a team."

Sebastian swallowed. He'd be working alongside magic users, psychics, whatever it was that Wendla and Francois could do. He was putting himself into deep danger, but of course... he was already in danger. The danger was chasing him, trying to hurt him.

Magic had caused this haunting, assuming Asher was to blame and there was no reason to doubt it.

But magic could also be its solution.

Kris stood up. "Take a minute. I'm going back to the house, to let the others know, and grab my tools."

"Thank you, Kris, will you be all right on your own?"

Kris nodded. "I won't look at the lawn, it'll be fine." They left.

Sebastian threw his arms around Basil and closed his eyes, squeezing him. Basil hugged him back.

"It's okay, love. I'll keep you safe. Stay by my side," Basil murmured softly.

Sebastian nodded. "I know you will. Magic... I'm processing it all, magic is just a tool, right? It's not inherently good or bad, it's...whoever wields it can make it do whatever. Bad people can make it to bad things, but good people can do good."

Basil squeezed him again. "That's right, and for what it's worth, I think there's more good than evil in the world."

Sebastian smiled. "Me too."

Basil

In the bedroom Basil stuffed his pockets with his deck of tarot cards, all the crystals he'd brought and the bundles of herbs.

Sebastian strapped a GoPro to his chest and was searching in the camera bag. The movements got more and more frantic. "No. No, no no ..."

"What's wrong?"

"I can't... the memory cards for the stuff I've already filmed, I can't find them. I know they were right here." Sebastian was frustrated, going into another bag.

"Did you back any of them up?" Basil asked.

"I haven't had time, last night I was too worried about you and today's been manic..." Sebastian knelt on the floor, bending to look under the bed and the desks, scrabbling at the rug. "They're gone. They're totally gone."

Basil sighed, touching Sebastian lightly on the shoulder. "Maybe one of the ghosts is trying to hide what happened?"

Sebastian sat back on his heels, panic melting into anger. "Those bastards. Take my memory cards? Now it's personal."

***

They met the others on the landing.

Wendla had a small hand mirror, and Francois held an old fashioned walking stick with a glass handle. Francois waved, apparently quite at ease with the goings on. "Heard you've had some adventures. Can't wait to get to the bottom of it."

Brit was there too. She held a dictaphone and an iron poker from the fireplace. She was grim-faced. "I don't ever want to hear a disembodied voice crying ever again, it's all I've heard since the parlour. It's following me room to room and there's nothing I can do. Let's end this."

Horatio was holding a torch and looking worried. "We can't all go up at once," they said. "The floor isn't reinforced and it's old. You have to stick to the cross beams, or you could fall through."

With that information on board they made their way up the stairs to the upper floor. Horatio led them to a back hallway, where a cord hung from the ceiling, almost in the corner of the Manor.

They tugged the cord and with a creak, an old step ladder unfolded from the ceiling.

A billow of dust accompanied the ladder. Horatio was ready for this and had covered their nose and mouth, but Basil and Sebastian beside him sneezed.

"I suppose I'd better go first so I can show you for safety," Horatio said.

"I'll be right behind you," Sebastian said. His GoPro was already recording.

Basil glanced at the others, Wendla and Francois looked interested, almost excited. Kris was clearly nervous, watching as Horatio made their way up the ladder. Brit's expression was all determination, her mouth a flat line.

Basil watched as Horatio and then Sebastian went into the gloom. The beam of Horatio's torch flicked here and there. Basil summoned another light orb and instructed it to follow Sebastian, keep him safe.

The small glowing light floated up the stairs and the gloom of the attic became slightly less.

"My turn, I suppose," Basil said, to try and jolly himself along. Now faced with a creepy, dusty old attic his earlier resolve and urgency faltered.

But his love was up there. He had to be there for Sebastian if no other reason.

It was enough to get him up the ladder and into the dimness.

Horatio's torch beam was lighting up the floor at his feet. "Stick to the crossbeams." They swept the light to and fro, mapping out the grid of solid wood beams on the floor. They sat above the plasterboard that must make up the ceiling, providing a gangway of sorts through the attic.

Placing his feet carefully, Basil made his way towards Sebastian, walking only on the beams.

The ceiling of the attic sloped dramatically at the edges but the space they were in was large, broken up by brick chimneys, and precarious stacks of boxes here and there. There was a strange shape in the far corner, Basil sent another light towards it and it resolved into a stack of old, broken chairs.

Kris emerged next, Horatio repeating the crossbeams instructions.

"If it wasn't for the dust it'd almost be pleasant up here," Sebastian said.

"I'm glad it doesn't seem to be full of rats," Basil said.

"Never had a rat problem in the manor," Horatio said, from across the way. "Maybe all the ghosts scare them off?"

Wendla and Francois walked boldly down the middle of the attic, balancing expertly on crossbeams as if they were professional tightrope walkers.

Brit brought up the rear, clutching the dictaphone and muttering into it.

Basil's chest swelled with a familiar pride. He was with a community again. This wasn't his witch coven, or his family, but a weird collection of experts who had somehow agreed to work together to face the cause of his haunting. Everyone shuffled into position, making a loose circle without being told to. Basil smiled, he'd better give them some guidance.

His orbs floated outside the circle, giving soft illumination and he added two more so the light was even.

"Right-oh, everyone, we're going to speak directly to the spirits and see what they have to say. Please ready your tools and I'll do a basic invocation with a charged crystal."

He felt in his pocket, letting his fingers roam through the crystals until the correct one presented itself. A spear shaped piece of smoky quartz. Protection, grounding, focus of negative energy in order to remove it? Perfect.

He pushed his magic into the crystal, and set his intention out loud.

"Here in this circle we invoke the restless spirits of Beach House. Let yourselves be known and seen. Those of us living in the circle are safe from harm, protected by the highest divine power, however the individual interprets that. So it is."

"With Papatuanuku's blessing, so it is," Sebastian said, his voice low and reverent.

"By the Goddess of the moon, so it is," Kris intoned.

"By the power of the universe, so it is," Wendla said next. Francois echoed her words.

Brit hesitated.

Basil caught her gaze, seeing her reluctance, and nodded his encouragement. "Whatever you set stock in," he said, low.

"By the laws of physics, so it is." Brit stood up straighter.

"By the spirits of my ancestors, so it is," Horatio said, to complete the circle.

Basil held the crystal aloft and projected his voice. Maybe he was showing off just a little for the camera, maybe. "Speak to us now, show us what troubles you!"

The attic returned to silence.

Basil took a breath, whatever was going to happen, it would happen in its own time.

The ring of people shifted, people looking around, growing impatient.

"I'm not entirely sure—" Francois started to say, but he stopped again.

There in the middle of the circle was a hanged man.

He swung gently, his clothing of the same era as the other ghosts Basil and the others had witnessed.

Brit spoke very fast into the dictaphone. "The image of a dead man, hanging by the neck on a piece of rope, either lynched or suicide I can't say."

"What is your name?" Wendla took a step forward, balancing easily on the crossbeam and bending to try and meet the eyes of the head, which lolled forward.

"Be careful," Kris said. "I can feel power building, it's like a lightning storm gathering."

Basil glanced at Kris, who had a ball of string in one hand, the other making knots.

"We would help you to your rest," Wendla said. "If you'd speak."

Basil's orbs and Horatio's torch went out and the room was plunged into darkness.

"Don't like that!" Brit exclaimed.

The room shuddered, knocking coming from below now.

Kris spoke a few words of French and the attic lit up again, bright as day.

"On the ceiling!" Sebastian said.

The hanged man hadn't moved, except the gentle swaying of the rope. But scrawled on the beams of the roof were the words "*He made me do it.*"

"Is that blood?" Kris asked.

As if waiting for that very question, the words began to smear and run, thick red blood dripping down.

"Wendla, ask if it's Hugh," Basil suggested.

"Hugh? Are you Hugh Crane?" Wendla put her hand on the corpse's hand and lifted it.

Another shudder. Basil grabbed onto Sebastian's arm to stay steady. Brit braced against the sloping ceiling.

"I am Hugh Crane!" The corpse twisted, grabbing Wendla by both her shoulders as it shouted, the voice dry and deep. "I am cursed to remain!"

Despite the horror-movie actions of a dead thing, Wendla kept remarkably cool. She lifted one eyebrow and blew out the corner of her mouth, as if expelling cigarette smoke.

"Well, I am Wendla Bergman and I hereby banish the curse on you, dear. You're free, you can go wherever you need to."

There was a terrible creaking sound as the house shuddered. It almost felt like it was lifting up from its foundations to shake itself off.

"He maaaaaade me do it!" Hugh groaned, the groan increased into a scream.

"I forgive you!" Wendla shouted.

The ghostly corpse of Hugh screamed, shaking Wendla bodily before swooping towards her, body transforming into smoky dust as it vanished into the roof.

Wendla staggered back in a swoon, her foot missing the cross beam and hitting the plasterboard below. Francois jumped forward to catch her, and they both crumpled to the floor.

"Careful!" Horatio cried.

Francois hurriedly lifted his wife off the uncertain flooring and draped her onto the crossbeams.

Basil took a deep breath and tuned into the atmosphere of Beach House. The shuddering had ceased, and as he breathed in the dusty air, he realised there was no oppressive feeling any longer.

Wendla had succeeded in moving on Hugh Crane's restless spirit and the house was just a house again.

Well, for the moment. They had no idea if Hugh's spirit was what was keeping Layla and the other children's ghosts around or not.

"Is she alright?" Basil asked.

Brit picked her way across the attic to examine Wendla. "Her heart-beat is faint but steady."

"Yes, yes a little fainting spell, she often gets them after exerting herself like that," Francois said. He stood, lifting his wife in his arms. "We'll be in our room, she usually comes back after an hour or so."

He walked confidently across the attic, sticking neatly to the cross-beams and descended the ladder with his wife over his shoulder.

"Gosh he's impressive," Basil murmured. "Both of them, really."

"So is that it then?" Horatio asked, hope bringing a lightness to their tone.

"We saw Layla Crane and some others on the lawn," Sebastian said.

"Hugh might have been holding them back," Basil said. "But that message, he made me... do you think he was talking about Asher?"

Kris nodded. "Well, that or he was blaming Satan but I don't know which is more likely."

"At any rate, I'd say we're done in the attic," Basil said.

"Let's get out of here and I'll see about some sandwiches for lunch," Horatio said.

Once they'd all descended, Horatio pushed the ladder back into the ceiling. They were heading downstairs when the distinct sound of a girl crying echoed over the group.

"There it is again!" Brit said. Her eyes were wide as she turned to Sebastian. "You hear it too, right?"

"Yes," he said. "It's okay, we'll find the source. If only I had my memory cards then I could review all the footage and find what we're missing."

"Let's hash it out together over lunch," Horatio said.

They sat in the parlour with filled rolls and tea sandwiches.

"When you were possessed, that horrible water gushed out your eyes," Sebastian said.

Basil chewed thoughtfully. "I can't remember much of that, but yes, there was water."

Sebastian continued, "and when whatever happened to me out there, the near-possession, I felt like I couldn't breathe, and my legs were weird too, like I couldn't move them the way I wanted."

"Maybe like you were in a confined space?" Basil suggested.

"Like the hidden passage in the chapel?" Kris asked. "Or the room in the library?"

"The what in the what now?" Horatio's eyes widened.

"Hidden rooms and passages," Basil said. "We found two, I'm sure there are more."

"Huh, cool." Horatio took a bite of their chicken filled roll.

Sebastian chewed on his pastrami roll and considered. "No, it was more constricting than those too."

"Layla said attic, which was where her father was." Brit consulted some handwritten notes. "What else did she say?"

"Asher's name. Which adds to the theory that it was his influence on Hugh... but what was the 'it' that he was referring to? Killing himself? Killing... someone else?" Sebastian suggested.

"More likely killing someone else," Kris said. "He said he was cursed, right? That could have been what Asher was doing to him."

"He certainly does like to cast curses." Basil glanced at Sebastian, remembering the horrible few hours he was a cat. "And being cruel."

"What about the journal?" Kris asked. "You said that the priest had concerns."

"Edmund described his father in a terrible rage, breaking up their gatherings." Basil recalled. He'd left the journal in the chapel for safekeeping but now he wished he'd brought it with him. "Edmund also seemed to know his own death was coming. He wrote that he knew Layla was in danger, but then it seemed to become all of them. People stopped coming to his sermons, so the badness must have been really pervasive, if strangers picked up on it."

He sighed and set down his egg salad sandwich to massage his temples.

"There's something else," Sebastian said, remembering an early interview. "Mindy said you took down the Crane family portraits, Horatio. Where did they get stored?"

"I sent them out for cleaning," Horatio said. "They came back wrapped in stuff, I stowed them in the library. You probably saw them stacked in the corner by the door."

Basil and Sebastian exchanged a look. Basil certainly hadn't noticed anything aside from the books and Sebastian shook his head, he hadn't noticed them either.

"There was weird activity in the library, but that was the secret room, not by the door. And I'm pretty sure that's where Asher stowed his books of magic… or maybe Hugh hid books he didn't approve of?"

"I don't think Hugh himself was doing any magic," Kris added.

"So, if we take for granted Hugh was working under Asher's influence, and he killed his children, what we need to do is find the bodies," Sebastian said.

"Out on the lawn where the picnic is?" Kris suggested.

Brit shook her head. "No, the water is the clue. And Sebastian felt he couldn't move... Horatio, is there a body of water nearby?"

"Aside from the ocean, at the foot of the cliff?" Horatio mused, tapping their finger on the arm of their chair. "No streams, or pools. Oh! But when I bought the place they said something about an old, boarded up well."

A horrible sinking feeling gripped Basil's stomach. "A well."

Sebastian gripped Basil's arm. "You dreamed you were drowning, that first night!"

"I'd forgotten, so much has happened since..." Basil shivered at the memory of the dream.

"I dream that pretty regularly, since I moved here," Horatio said. "It's horrible."

A door somewhere nearby slammed.

The sound of Layla's crying returned, louder than ever.

"Bingo," Sebastian said, without mirth.

CHAPTER THIRTEEN

SEBASTIAN

Horatio led the way out into the gardens, and all the way down to the edge of the property, where a rickety old wooden fence stood behind some trees. The grass here was overgrown and packed with weeds, tall dandelions and something that looked like nightshade.

Sebastian left his GoPro on but brought his usual camera as well.

"I know it was around here somewhere, must be hidden by the grass..." Horatio said. They walked up the border of trees, swishing a stick through the grass to find it.

Basil knelt in the grass and pulled three tarot cards. "Layla, can you tell me if we're close?"

Sebastian filmed over Basil's shoulder.

He flipped the first card, it showed a blindfolded woman holding a set of scales in one hand, a sword in the other. The meaning was justice in the traditional sense, someone being held accountable, balancing the scales.

"Justice," Basil said. "Yes, we're going to bring justice, balance to the property. You'll be able to go to rest, but we need to find the well." He flipped over the next card. A young knight was depicted riding a horse, holding up a chalice with a rose in it.

"The knight of cups..." he glanced over his shoulder at Sebastian. "A young person, creative and emotional..."

Brit was fossicking through the weeds, looking stern and serious.

Kris was swinging a pendulum on a string, and frowning at it.

Horatio had walked some ways off, and was kicking at the undergrowth, frustrated.

"Horatio," Sebastian breathed. "They're young, they invited us here because they were afraid, frustrated. They keep it in but I think they're really grateful we all came."

"You're close Horatio!" Basil called out.

Horatio turned to give him the thumbs up, then got deeper into the weeds, searching.

Kris and Brit moved to join Horatio, but Basil stayed on the ground.

Sebastian knew why, there was one more card to go. "What's the third card?"

Basil flipped the card, revealing the Hierophant, a stern man depicted as a bishop or cardinal, blessing a supplicant, a large stained glass window behind him. It meant higher education, institutions and knowledge. "A priest? Edmund, he must be close as well..."

"Did no one wonder where the family had gone?" Sebastian mused. "Usually there would be gravesites, tombstones..."

Basil shrugged and shuffled the three cards back into the deck. "It was a different time, I guess. New colonists. Not so many people out this way."

"Found it!" Horatio cried.

Basil and Sebastian hurried over. Kris, Brit and Horatio were busy clearing the weeds from a small mound, overgrown with moss. It was barely half a foot off the ground. It was nothing more than a small mortared opening with a moss-covered wooden lid nailed down to it.

They cleared a patch around it.

"We're not going to pull a body out of there like in *Ringu* are we?" Kris asked, their voice shaky.

"No. It'll be bones by now anyway," Basil said. "But we can release the spirit, and give her some peace with our words."

Sebastian handed Basil his camera, crouched beside the well and bent to examine it. "These nails look rusted through, should be easy enough to pull open."

"Pry it with this." Brit handed Sebastian the iron fireplace poker she'd been carrying. "It'll be easier with a lever."

Kris knelt to assist and Sebastian wedged the poker under the lid and applied pressure.

The lid came off with surprisingly little resistance.

The sound of crying echoed up from inside the well, more desperate now.

"Alone, so cold!" the words resounded alongside the sobs.

"You're not alone, now." Basil said, as clearly and strongly as he could manage. "Your father has moved on, we're about to find your brother, and you can be at rest."

The well overflowed with the same brackish water that had poured out of Basil's eyes.

Kris and Sebastian's knees and feet were soaked before they could move away. The water seeped out, horribly thick in appearance, almost like a slime.

"It's water, but it might be ectoplasm as well," Sebastian said. "Try not to touch it too much."

"Please, Layla!" Horatio burst out, their voice infused with sorrow. "Please, tell us how we can help you? I know your father was an asshole, mine is too, we have that in common. Please let me help?"

The water eased and receded into the well.

Kris groaned, a hand going to their head. "She's coming," Kris murmured.

The ground shuddered, the strength of a minor earthquake, and Layla rose up out of the well. She looked different now, her dress torn and water-logged, but her face was clear, even radiant. A wreath of wildflowers adorned her hair, which flowed loose around her shoulders. She held a doll in one arm, a weirdly realistic Victorian doll.

Layla looked directly at Horatio. "My father sought to quell my power, and he invited one in to eat it. My sister," she lifted her elbow, joggling the doll, "was soon consumed, too weak to resist, but I fought back. Thus, my fate..." she gestured with her other hand.

"You were witches?" Basil breathed.

Layla didn't look at him, barely acknowledged anyone but Horatio. "My power was too strong for my time. You are an iconoclast as well, refusing to be bound by small definitions. You are too strong to be quelled."

Horatio made a soft whimpering noise. Sebastian kept the camera focused on the ghost of Layla, but stole a glance at Horatio, who had tears streaming down their face.

"We are not our fathers. We're stronger than they are," Horatio said, their voice thick with emotion.

Layla nodded. "That's correct. Take your power and flourish, fill Beach House with friends, parties, art and music. That will chase out any poor feeling that remains."

Sebastian nudged Basil. "You should offer them both crystals."

"Oh yes," Basil dug in his pocket and withdrew a handful of stones. He held his hand out to Horatio and Layla. "Please, take one or more of these, to help you."

Slowly, Layla broke her gaze with Horatio to look over the offerings. Layla nodded and a piece of pink crystal lifted out of Basil's palm and flew to her. It embedded in the centre of her chest.

Horatio watched this, and then looked at the remaining crystals, choosing another pink one. Quartz, Sebastian thought.

"Thank you, all," Layla said, her voice quieter. "My brother is over the cliff. Please send him a crystal as well, he will be grateful. His bones are long gone but his spirit lingers."

"Thank you, Layla," Horatio said. "I won't forget you, not ever. And I'll do what you say, I'll make Beach House live again."

Layla smiled, her flower crown burst into a flurry of butterflies, and she was gone.

Kris hugged Horatio as they sobbed.

The butterflies flitted about the heads of those gathered, and then disappeared as well.

The group stood in respectful silence, some dabbing at their eyes, as Horatio cried. Finally they straightened, pulled back from Kris' embrace and wiped their eyes. "I'm ready."

"Excellent work," Basil said. "The dead must be mourned." He pocketed all but one of the crystals. "Now, if we send Edmund off with this and a few words, the job should be done."

"What's that crystal?" Sebastian asked.

"This is clear quartz," Basil said. "Horatio took rose quartz for unconditional love, and Layla has pink kunzite for love and compassion. She put it right into her heart chakra... I think she really was a witch."

Sebastian slipped his camera into his shoulder bag, shut off the GoPro and hooked his arm through Basil's. "I think I know just the place to do this." He led them to the path behind the house, where he'd hesitated at the cliff's edge.

"So, I think what happened was, Asher influenced Hugh and Hugh drowned his daughters in the well," Horatio said. "Edmund tried to stop him, but got pushed off the cliff."

Kris nodded. "Then when Asher had no one else to feed off?"

"He left, and Hugh was overcome with remorse," Horatio sighed. "It's awful. No wonder the house has been so full of pain."

They found their way to the cliff's edge and stood in a cluster, a group of mourners paying their last respects.

"I'm sorry for what happened, Edmund," Basil said, after a lengthy silence. "Your sisters and your father have moved on, you don't need to protect anyone any more. Move on, and be at peace."

He tossed the clear quartz over the cliff. Somewhere nearby a seagull cried, a long, lonely sound.

They stayed like that for a few minutes, simply breathing in the salt spray and thinking everything over.

Sebastian thought of the terrible waste, the family destroyed simply at Asher's whim. Now, at least, he had played a part in putting them all to rest. Part of his fear had gone to rest as well, he thought.

Between them all, such a disparate group of folks, they'd done something incredible. Sebastian took Basil's hand and squeezed it. It felt correct. He felt something he wasn't sure he'd ever feel again. Euphoria from doing something in line with his life's calling. To find ghosts, discover their stories, and do what he could to help. He wasn't all the way back to his old self, but he'd taken an important step.

Finally, Horatio clapped their hands. "No time like the present! I'll get Andrew cooking something fine. Let's have a party tonight and chase out the cobwebs!"

"I'll go check on the Bergmans," Brit said. "Catch them up on everything."

Horatio and Brit walked off. Kris lingered. "You two are great fun," they said. "How can we stay in touch?"

"We'll work something out, even if it's letters in the post," Basil said.

Kris headed back inside, satisfied, leaving Basil and Sebastian arm in arm, side by side on the edge of a cliff.

"Another mystery solved."

"Indeed, Watson, and what a curious case it was." Basil arched one eyebrow and grinned.

Sebastian snorted. "I'm Watson? I don't know about that."

Basil leaned his head on Sebastian's shoulder. "I do. You're steadfast, loyal, good in a fight and you always know what to say. I'm the weirdo with a special gift."

Sebastian slipped his arms around Basil and kissed his forehead. "You're *my* weirdo."

"Forever and ever." Basil tilted his chin up and kissed Sebastian.

Even though they must have shared a thousand kisses, Sebastian's heart still sped up.

"Forever and ever."

EPILOGUE

BASIL

True to their word, Horatio had thrown an amazing party. Eve had roasted a turkey, trays of roast vegetables, fresh bread, Yorkshire puddings and rich, tasty gravy.

The champagne had flowed, helped in no small part by the Bergman's skill with mixing cocktails and to be perfectly honest, Basil couldn't remember everything that had gone on that night.

There had definitely been karaoke with the assistance of Sebastian's phone and Bluetooth speaker.

He wasn't entirely sure if a dance off had followed, although he did remember Wendla and Brit doing a tango on the dining table, for some reason.

The next morning, Basil went to the kitchen, brewed up his father's hangover remedy and served it to everyone over breakfast.

Once they were all sufficiently recovered, thanks to the potion, Horatio stood up.

"My heartful... no, wait. Heartfelt thanks to all of you," they said. "You didn't know what you were getting into, but you came out here anyway. I want to offer you a reward of some kind."

"Oh no need for that, dear," Wendla said, flapping her hand. "We have plenty of money."

"Speak for yourself," Brit said.

"Perhaps there's something you'd like to take from the Manor?" Horatio said. "Although of course, money is an option as well."

Basil blinked. "You do have rather a lot of magic books in the library's hidden room. Some of them rather dangerous, I'd be happy to take those off your hands."

"Done, help yourself," Horatio said.

"I just want my memory cards back," Sebastian said. "Don't suppose anyone seen them?"

"Oh these?" Brit produced a handful of small black cartridges. "I found them on the stairs leading to my room last night. I was going to ask if anyone was missing them."

"Thank you!" Sebastian took the memory cards and clutched them to his chest. "Thank you Layla!"

"Money would be great," Brit said. "I'm always looking for funding."

"Cash is always welcome," Kris nodded. "But uh, maybe you wouldn't mind if I also stayed on a few more days?"

Horatio smiled softly, their cheeks pinking just a little. Basil wondered if there was something sparking between them.

"Stay as long as you like, Kris. If you want you could bring your familiar here. I'm sure you miss him, and I'd love to meet him."

"Maybe I will," Kris ducked their head, smiling wide.

"Nothing for us," Francois said. "But the contact details for each of you, you simply must come to our next party. Those dance moves, Basil, I must see them again."

Basil blushed and focused on his breakfast.

"Okay, if you want to nominate a charity let me know, as well," Horatio said. "I'm happy to divert some funds. And finally, all of you are welcome back here any time. You'll get invites to all my parties from here on out."

Over the next few minutes, everyone finished eating and made their way back to their rooms to pack the last of their things. They moved slowly, lingering perhaps over last conversations and promises to stay in touch.

Wendla and Francois kissed Basil and Sebastian on both cheeks, embraced them tight, and loaded their bags into their car. Wendla stuck her head out the passenger window. "We'll see you soon, darlings! That's a Bergman promise!"

They tooted the horn as they drove off.

Brit hurried down the stairs with her bags. "See you, thank you for the talk when I was panicking!" Brit paused. Her expression dropped. "I'm really sorry about my attitude at the start of all this. I came in with my mind made up, and I think I was a bit of an asshole about it."

"Thank you," Basil said. He opened his arms and Brit hugged him.

"The fact that you actually did change your mind, and then were right there beside us? That speaks volumes about your character, Brit." Sebastian hugged her next.

"Okay. You have my card, yes? I'll be off then. I have to get this all written up while it's fresh in the memory!" Brit grabbed her bags off the floor and went out to her car.

Horatio lingered by the door while Basil and Sebastian retrieved their bags and brought them down.

"Well, I guess we're on our way, too," Basil said.

"Thank you for the invitation, it means a lot to be thought of that way," Sebastian added.

"I believe the tribal elders are on their way," Horatio said. "If you'd like to stay for the blessing, you're welcome to."

"Oh, I'd actually love that. Do you mind, Basil?" Sebastian's sparkled as he met his eyes.

Basil nodded. "Sure, sounds like fun."

Horatio seemed to relax.

Looking at the door frame, Basil blinked. The wards. He'd felt the wards on the way in, worn down and barely functional. "Horatio, would you mind if I fix up the wards on the door? I'll put in new protections for you."

"Sure," Horatio said. "That'd be grand. If you can make this entire place feel as safe as the chapel?"

"I'll try," Basil said. "Though I think the blessing will do most of that work."

He pressed his hand to the door frame and drew up his magic, feeling the purple flow through him and into the solid timber. He willed the wards back to life, and rewrote them in his mind's eye, blending the protections that Layla had put there so many years before with his own version of them. It didn't take more than a few seconds, but when he pressed the wards into the wood, it felt like he'd been elsewhere for a while.

"There, that should do it." Basil shook off the feeling and turned to smile at Horatio. "Get in touch if you ever want them updated, I'll be happy to come out and do it again."

"Thank you, Basil."

The representatives of the local marae drove up shortly after Basil and Sebastian had stowed their bags in their car.

They were all dressed in black, and a few had white feathers in their hair. A woman with a walking stick and Ta Moko tattooed on her chin approached first, the others following.

"Welcome," Horatio said. "Thank you for coming out."

"Looks like some progress has been made," the woman said. "My name is Tui, I'll be leading the karakia. I'll start now, we need to walk the entirely house, please follow behind quietly."

"Ready now, auntie?" One of the younger man asked.

Tui nodded and looked up at the house. She began to chant in Te Reo, her voice rising and falling as she stepped through the door and inside.

The young man who had spoken walked a step behind her, along with the young woman and the older man who had arrived as well. Tui had the gravitas of a matriarch. The others deferred to her as the prayed for peace and cleansed the house spiritually.

The others walked behind, slow and silent. Horatio, Kris, Basil and Sebastian fell in behind them.

The process was slow and meditative, giving Basil time to reflect on everything that had happened over the last few days.

The library, where they'd had their first verification that something magical was involved. He checked the corners but could see no evidence of the Crane family portraits. Perhaps Horatio had moved them?

They visited each room on the ground floor, then made their way up the stairs.

It was there Basil saw the Crane family portraits had been hung on the wall – it must have been Andrew's job for the morning. Horatio noticed Basil looking at them and smiled.

They toured each of the bedrooms, Horatio coming forward with keys when needed. Basil rather enjoyed seeing all the different rooms, not so different to the one he'd stayed in, but each with different colour themes.

The last few days had been intense, but this felt like the correct way to end it all. Blessing the space, observing by walking it, and giving it respect at the same time.

Basil's entire being felt at peace, in tune with the universe, and the house itself felt warm too. The threatening aura was entirely gone and the rooms felt warmer.

On the top floor Tui paused, and looked skeptically at the hatch in the ceiling. Then she turned to the group behind her and nodded, just once, with emphasis. "It's done."

The young woman handed Horatio a fern frond. "Keep this in the house, okay?"

"Of course," Horatio said. "Please, if you'd like refreshments I've got tea and coffee, and cakes and things, by way of thanks."

"Yes, thank you." Tui's stern features held a moment longer and then she broke into a grin. "Got any chocolate eclairs on offer?"

"I'm sure we can find something. Come down to the parlour, and take a seat."

Downstairs Basil and Sebastian exchanged a look and decided between them not to linger further.

"We'll take off, get out of your hair," Sebastian said to Horatio as Tui and her attendants settled in.

Horatio pulled him in to a hug. "Thank you, you kept everything so grounded even while... all of it happened."

"It's truly my pleasure," Basil said. He hugged Kris next.

"Stay in touch," Kris said. "Or I'll come invade your library."

"You should anyway. You'd like the magical books collection."

"Thank you for having us," Sebastian ran his hand through his hair . "It really helped me process some stuff, being here, meeting everyone."

"I'm glad." Horatio and Kris waved from the door, then disappeared inside.

Sebastian put on one of his chill playlists and they were silent as they drove up the driveway and away from Beach House.

"You're really feeling better?" Basil asked, once they were back on the main road.

"I think so," Sebastian said. "I feel stronger. I'm not entirely over my fears, I don't think I ever will be, but I can still get stuff done. Do my job, summon ghosts and all."

Basil leaned his head back against the chair, relief and bittersweet happiness mingling with something more determined. "Good. Because you know what we have to do next?"

"Get home?" Sebastian suggested.

"No. well, yes, but...not what I meant."

"What did you mean?"

"We're going to have to track down Asher."

Sebastian sighed, and then nodded. "Yes, you're right. He could be preying on another family right now."

Basil looked out over the landscape as it sped by. "We have a lot of resources we can tap into, and together, I think we can beat him for good. Are you up for it?"

Sebastian put his hand on Basil's knee, Basil took it and threaded their fingers together.

Sebastian grinned. "You know I am. We're unstoppable, aren't we?"

— to be continued

Also By

Jamie Sands

Stay in touch by subscribing to my newsletter
https://greykelpiestudio.eo.page/tk5gx

Mt Eden Witches

Overdues and Occultism

Monsters and Manuscripts

Rituals and Roadtrips

YA novella: Onesies and Ouijaboards

Detective Duarte Mysteries

he Other Side of the Mirror

Reactionary Bewitchment

Monster Slayers (Young adult)

The Suburban Book of the Dead

The Suburban Book of Dreams

Romantic Comedies

Four Years and Today

BEAcon of Love

Finding Tane

  Under Jaxon Knight

  Santa's Sacking

Rival Princes

Mischief and Mayhem

Recipe for Chaos

The Good, The Bad and The Dad

The Trouble with Order

Short story collections

This Unusual Life!

Some Things That Don't Make Sense